The Chase

Begins

CATASTROPHE INCOMING: VOLUME I

AIMEE DONNELLAN

THE CHASE BEGINS

Cover art by: Katelyn McNeely

Cover design by: Marten Norr

Editor: Quinton Li (www.quintonli.com)

www.aimeedonnellan.com

The 'Catastrophe Incoming' series

Books 6-12 to be published in 2025 and onward, exact months to be confirmed.

Contents

For everyone who has a hunger for knowledge burning deep within them,
and those who will never, ever be satisfied.

Content Warnings and Image Descriptions

The following work contains: frequent coarse language, descriptions of violence, descriptions of blood, mild sexual references, a claustrophobic situation, descriptions of murder, arson, suffocation, and a complicated toxic relationship.

Image Description Text for Book Cover

A sunset sky background covered in stars and a band of green magic, sets the scene for an androgynous figure standing strong. They have one hand grasping a large book to their person while their other hand is illuminated with golden magic. Their clothes are a simple dark trenchcoat, shirt, and tartan trousers. Their skin is medium brown while their dark brown hair blows in a breeze to one side, revealing the hairless, golden scaled left side of their head. Their left eye is bright green and draconic in nature, with green scales surrounding it — in great contrast to their brown eye on the right. Their expression is resolute and pensive.

The text reads: The Chase Begins, Aimee Donnellan, and Catastrophe Incoming Volume I

Image Description Text for Map of Kequm (following page)

A city map detailing a city emcompassed by roughly circular walls, but showing some building and farmland on the outskirts. A river runs through the western side of the city, coming from the north and meeting the body of water at the south end. The only labelled features in the city are the following:

Northwest section: Tower of Justice, Temple of the Judge, Temple of the Warbringer

North section: Temple of the Battle Maiden, Temple of the Scholar

East section: Temple of the Everflame, Temple of the Life Giver

South Section: Temple of the First Inventor, Temple of the Winter Wolf

CITY OF KEQUM

Temple of The
Warbringer

Temple of The
Battle Maiden

...ver of
...stice

Temple of the
Scholar

Temple of The
Judge

Temple of The
Everflame

Temple of The
Life Giver

Temple of The
First Inventor

Temple of The
Winter Wolf

Dramatis Personae

In order of appearance

Lark - *they/them* - A Seeker of the Scholar

Wren - *she/her* - A gentle warrior

Cillian - *he/they* - The emergency admin of Kequm

Andrian - *he/him* - The Deputy Bishop of the Scholar

Nightingale - *she/her* - An ex-Seeker turned murderer

Palla - *she/her* - Champion of the Bishops and follower of War

NOTE: They/them pronouns, as when used when referring to a person of unknown gender, can also be used to refer to someone who is more comfortable not aligning with womanhood or manhood specifically or entirely, such as Lark.

<u>Gods of the Higher Pantheon</u>

The Winter Wolf - God of Winter, the Moon, and the Ocean

The Life Giver - Goddess of Spring, Nature, and Growth

The Everflame - God of Summer, Light and Fire

The First Inventor - Goddess of Autumn, Air and Change

The Warbringer - God of War, Destruction, and Chaos

The Judge - Goddess of Justice, Righteousness and Mercy

The Trickster - God of Mischief, Tricks and Shadows

The Scholar - God of Study and Knowledge, brother to the Battle Maiden

The Battle Maiden - Goddess of Strategy, Battle and Wisdom, sister to the Scholar

Chapter 1

THE FIRST SHIMMER OF magic through the sky interrupts a mouthful of fried bread and a convoluted story about a drunk wyvern.

"Did you see that?" Lark asks, to check that the flash of blue hadn't been their dragon eye playing tricks on them.

"See what?"

Gravy stains Wren's chin from how quickly she has devoured her own bread, and her face is still caught in laughter. It should be a crime to look away from something so wonderful and yet —

Lark glances up. The sky is clear now, and they mourn the days when they could trust their first impression of the world around them. The market they are standing in is full of people who haven't paused and are continuing to shop and chat.

"Come on, what happened after it got kicked out of the vineyard?" Wren asks.

"Oh, I offered it a lift, wherever it wanted," Lark says, snapping back to attention with a grin. "It didn't exactly have faith in my mode of transport, but it told me about its home nest in specific detail. And off we went."

"And *that's* how you ended up in a snowbank."

"And *that's* how I ended up in a snowbank."

Wren shakes her head as another laugh rocks her body. "I don't know why I believe you. Ever."

"Because you know it's true!"

"But it shouldn't be! So why do I believe you?"

Lark blinks at her. "Well, I'm told I have a very honest face. When people aren't put off by the dragon eye, that is."

"One day, you're going to tell me how you got that."

Lark grins, if only to hide the sting of the memory in question. They push down the voice that had coaxed them into it, any and all memory of that voice and the person it belongs to.

"Oh, Wren. You wouldn't believe me if I told you," they say. That part is truthful enough.

A flash above them — magic like crushed sapphire in an arc, revealing the dome shape of the city wards. Horns start blaring and a hush falls over the marketplace, followed by a wave of uncertainty and hesitation. A moment later, people begin to disperse at top speed. Fearful whispers of dragons linger in the empty spaces.

"Alright. *That* one, I saw," Wren says, gaping. "Are they right? A dragon, incoming?"

A dragon would make the most sense in the current war climate. Lark's hometown, being in fact the holiest city of the Theocracy and the most westward city, is a crucial and dangerous location. And in their entire time in the city, they have only heard the horns once, when the first dragon attack had seen a massive creature of ocean blue scales decimate a quarter of the city.

"It can't be a dragon," Lark says, licking their lips, their hands beginning to gesture excitedly, "by all logic, the only danger *should* be a dragon, but... they've just changed the wards to *inward*."

"So it's not just *not* a dragon," Wren says, voice slow, "it's something serious enough... they're leaving us exposed *to* dragons. What could that even be?"

"I have no idea!" A laugh escapes Lark's throat, inappropriate and delighted. "I love not knowing."

Wren snorts. "You *hate* not knowing."

"I love the not knowing that comes *before* the knowing, Wren, or else there would be no cause to be excited about knowing anything in the first place. Although there is something to be said for the acquisition of knowledge you never *knew* you were lacking—"

"Lark," Wren says with fond amusement, "possible crisis. Do you have a plan?"

Lark runs a hand through their chin length dark hair, eyes darting around the city and mentally mapping routes and destinations before returning to Wren's face. "Well, we could head to the ward hub and see what additional information was passed on with the order to invert the wards. The temple of War is bound to know something, and my own temple is of course in the know by nature—"

Wren's eyes have drifted beyond Lark's shoulder. "Or we could ask that city official who seems to be headed straight for us."

Lark whirls around. A well dressed person bearing the city office crest is striding towards them with purpose, flanked by a pair of guards. They are talking animatedly to the guards as they walk and getting little in return. A long braid of white blonde hair comes past their partly elven ears and hangs over their shoulder, while their red and cream robes mark them as a follower of the Everflame, God of Summer and Fire.

"Seeker Lark!" they call out. "Wonderful to meet you in person." They offer a hand in greeting, and when Lark takes it they shake vigorously. "The name's Cillian. Emergency admin."

"Good to meet you," Lark says, returning their hands to their trouser pockets. "What can I do for you? There must be something going on if you've inverted the wards."

Cillian grins as an odd, possibly nervous laugh escapes them. "One could say. I've been asked to escort you to the Tower of Justice. Your assistance is required."

"Of course, of course. What's got everyone so spooked that you need my insight? Or do you need me to read somebody?"

Cillian's eyes flick to Lark's left one for a moment. It's peculiar, to be better known for one's body part than one's work, at least half of the time.

"Better that you just come, I think," Cillian says. "Follow me."

With that he turns and begins walking northwestward. Lark's feet scuffle in the dirt in a dance of excitement, and they turn on the spot to grin at Wren.

"Mysterious summons, no explanation other than *come and see*?" they say. "These ones are my *favourite*."

Wren chuckles. "One day I'll get used to how you react to a crisis. Will I need my sword?"

"Oh, probably!"

Lark grabs her by the hand and pulls her along. It's fortunate she tends to follow Lark happily at any given point because shifting her tall, solid frame by force would be a near impossible task. They're a good fit — a mage and a warrior, content to travel side by side learning what new things they can and fixing problems they encounter.

It should be enough. But there is something behind Wren's green eyes, some deeper plan or thought she does not share.

You hate not knowing, Wren had said, and she is right. But there are worse things. Lark has not asked in the near half year they have known each other; as long as the question goes unanswered, the answer cannot leave Lark as the only one without purpose or direction. A seeker of nothing at all.

And so, Wren is welcome to her privacy. *That's why she wears the flower crown. The flowers are full of secrets.*

Amused by the thought, and realising how much of the city they are missing with this change in direction, Lark tugs on Wren's hand to point afar and resume the verbal tour they had been giving before the snack break.

"So all the Temples are arranged by function of course, with the Winter Wolf down south ways by the lake," Lark says, "and the Life Bringer out by the farms. There, that way — you see that building over on the north side? That's the university, with my temple attached."

"For the Scholar, makes sense," Wren says, glancing at the symbol of the scroll, book and quill that hangs on a chain around their neck. "Gods, you don't half make the temples huge, do you? So that's where you studied?"

"That's the place, yes, and then the martial training academy attached to the temple of the Battle Maiden alongside, of course."

"Of course," Wren says, as the pairing of the sibling gods is common in any country that worships the Higher Pantheon, not just Lark's particularly devout one. "I'm guessing that's the Tower of Justice."

The tower in question lies before them, growing taller with every step they take, looming over the city with its juxtaposition of the white stone and the shadow it casts. Attached to the Temple of the Judge, the Goddess of Justice and Righteousness, it holds the appropriate multitudes within.

Lark swallows hard at the thought of the last time they had been inside. The upper levels, the ones that see daylight, are devoted to those who have committed crimes but shown great promise and attitude towards atonement and redemption. Lark is more familiar with the underground section — where more hope dies with every foot between the occupant and daylight.

"That's one hell of a prison," Wren says, with a mixture of awe and distaste. "Also... can we go back to the market when we're done? If that's alright?"

So you can question more people when you think I'm distracted?
Lark is tempted to ask. They do not.

"Of course," they say instead, with a pleasant smile.

Cillian ushers them into the tower's entry level. It is a large, pleasant space with doors leading the way into the lawhouse on the left and the processing hold on the right. Another, smaller but more embellished, is the temple connection. The administration desk is empty, at least until Cillian hurries to get back behind it, but one figure is leaning over it and poring across papers clipped to a board. Upon Cillian rushing past them, the figure looks up.

"Andrian!" Lark says with delight. "It's been years."

"Indeed," Andrian says, as stiff as Lark recalls him ever being. Graduating from the Scholar's Keep alongside Lark and their other classmates had done little to relieve the human man from a countenance that gives him the look of someone expecting a surprise exam sprung on them at any moment. His green eyes, cupped in exhausted shadow, consider Lark from under bushy brown brows and an amusingly practical cropped haircut. "You're... cheery, under the circumstances, even for you."

Lark blinks. They cannot help feeling like with each stride into the tower and every word spoken they are descending a staircase further and further into the dark and a missing step or sudden ending is going to catch them. "Circumstances? I haven't been *told* the circumstances, Andrian. I was summoned and so I came."

"Why didn't you *tell* them?" Andrian asks Cillian with bewilderment.

Cillian is busy shuffling papers and glances up, their delicate brows arching. "I wasn't aware that it was my place, Seeker Seer. It's a delicate situation."

Andrian sighs and rubs his temples. "You'd better follow me, Lark."

There is a part of Lark, the moment they are led to the spiral staircase that takes one to the underground floors, that guesses what is coming before any more can be said. It is the rational part, the spark of irrefutable genius that has gotten them this far in every endeavour.

But that part is a fraction of its usual size and has been since they had entered the tower. Because it doesn't matter if it fits, it doesn't matter if all the evidence points to it, it cannot be the truth.

One floor down. Then again. Headed all the way to the bottom, to the least repentant. That tiny part of Lark screams louder as they recognise the path in reverse, remembers walking it with nausea and heartbreak threatening to choke them.

They try to say Andrian's name but cannot. He is walking ahead, so Lark grabs him by the arm and forces him to look back.

"Andrian, *please*," they say, in that instant near deranged with uncertainty and dread. "Tell me. Is she—"

The rest of the question dies in their throat. They have reached the bottom of the stairs and Lark's foot meets even ground unexpectedly, their body going haywire with instinctive surprise. Combined with what they see before them, it is enough to stumble and only Wren's sure hands save them.

"Gods," her low voice whispers behind them, "what happened here?"

Bodies litter the floor. All guards, armoured and bloodless. One barred cell door at the end hangs open.

"Nightingale," Lark says, to no one at all. The single word, the name, is all at once a caress, a damnation, and a prayer. "She's escaped. Gods help us all."

Chapter 2

LARK'S BODY IS NOT built for such a war of alarm, conflict and stress as the one waging within their chest at this moment. They can barely focus enough to look at Andrian and form words.

"How did this happen?!"

"It seems she overwhelmed the anti-magic shackles. We're not sure how—"

Lark steps through the obstacle course of bodies to stare into the cell. The walls are blank but for a few doodles and equations. *Why did I expect something different? I delivered notebooks myself.*

"—it should be impossible, of course."

"Yes, Andrian, because she truly has a history for caring about what rules to follow, legal or logical or laws of the known universe," Lark all but snaps, with the smallest of glances his way. They crouch in front of the broken shackles on the ground and run their hand over the metal.

Images flash through their mind at rapid speed. *Metal in a forge being moulded and hammered. The dozens of people whose wrists have borne the shackles. Magic, audacious and wrong and too powerful, exploding and shattering that which it should never have been able to touch.*

Lark releases the shackles and swallows. They make their way back to the stairs. "She found a way. She always does. Moving on. How long ago did this happen? Why bother bringing us down here, why not just *tell* me, every second she's free everyone in this city is in danger!"

Andrian coughs, a frown of concern in danger of being permanently pressed into his eyebrows. "I... Lark, to be honest, I didn't know the best way to tell you. You're a credit to our temple and profession, but this is—"

"I am not the priority here! Up, back up, all of us, now!"

Lark hurries both humans back up the stairs as their heart beats against their chest so violently it hurts. As they come into the foyer again, Wren finds her voice.

"Lark, what's going on? Who did all of that?"

"Nightingale," Lark, Andrian and Cillian at the desk all say in the same instant. It is followed by their individual elaborations.

"A murderous, fascinating individual." Cillian.

"An example of the search for knowledge gone wrong." Andrian.

"A powerful, complicated problem." Lark.

Wren considers all of the explanations and crosses her arms. "But they want you specifically, and you look like you're going to be sick. Why?"

Lark sighs and rubs their temples. The dark yellow and brown of Andrian's anxiety is flaring in their vision, while Wren's befuddlement and alarm have created a beautiful swirl of bright turquoise around her. It is not helping Lark keep a straight head — a near impossible thing where Nightingale is concerned already.

"Because I helped bring her in the first time," they say, "because she used to be my friend, because if she's out then we need to put anything we were thinking about doing aside. She's one of the most dangerous people alive right now."

A silence follows. One of Lark's favourite things about Wren is the time she takes to think, to process, to consider her words before letting them loose. Lark throws out words like erratic melodies tripping over themselves to reach a crescendo in a finale — Wren speaks like a ballad.

"Well, shit."

Lark in any other situation would have smiled at how much gravitas she can give the words.

"I see what you mean about a powerful, complicated problem," she says. "How did it go from friendship to..." She hesitates, eyes flicking to Cillian. The fact that she doesn't say the word *murder* aloud makes Lark want to kiss her. Probably platonically. "Everything else?"

Andrian coughs. "She attended the university with Lark and I." He shakes his head, the picture of disappointment. "Brilliant, undoubtedly. But while her research certainly took her in some unconventional directions, she never gave any indication of the psychosis that would come later."

Psychosis is not how Lark would describe it. That, however, is getting into territory that Lark has no intention of sharing with any official of the city, not even an old friend. Their memory burns with flashing light and magic and shouting, and for a moment it feels as though their veins are boiling from the inside, as if the rogue magic within them is flexing and laughing at Lark's lack of control.

"She gained power that tempted her away from morality," Lark says. Speaking of it like a diagnosis, like an incident they didn't witness, feels wrong. But all of it is wrong. "And away from those of us who would not abandon it."

"So you'll lead the search for her, then, Lark? Bring her back, as you did before?" Andrian asks.

"Provided you can find a more accomplished enchanter for your mage shackles," Lark says, perhaps unkindly, but to Andrian's credit he doesn't so much as blink.

"Of course."

Lark glances at Wren. "I should probably go alone. I can't guarantee your safety. In fact, I can guarantee a *lack* of safety."

"I keep *you* safe," Wren argues.

"Not with her—"

"Lark, I've fought bandits, monsters, all sorts. I can look after myself."

"No one is invincible, Wren, she has killed people more powerful than you before—"

"Power isn't everything," Wren says. "Plenty of powerful things don't have brains. Or common sense. I do."

Lark's mouth closes when no immediate retort comes out of it. Wren holds their gaze, more serious than they have seen her in days.

"You don't get to use my strength just when it's convenient," she says. "You made me care about you. And your safety. The consequence is my loyalty. Whether you want it or not. I'm coming."

Lark's cheeks flush at the unexpected declaration. It is lovely, it is wonderful, it is altogether too much with everything else happening and simply will not fit in their head or heart the way it should. With their head dipped, no words come.

Wren's hand covers their arm and squeezes, drawing their gaze back to her. Her eyes are determined as anything, and fiercely tender.

"I'm no reckless Seeker," she says softly, for their ears only. "I take care where I step. I'm coming. Now. Together?"

"Together," they agree, covering her hand with theirs and squeezing it back.

"Your locative magic will be enough to find her, Lark, I trust?" Andrian asks.

"Locative magic?" Lark blinks at him. "Well, naturally, Andrian, but I don't need locative magic to find her. It's obvious where she would go."

"Is it? She's difficult to predict."

"Not especially, you've locked the entire city down to ensure she cannot escape, yes?" Lark barely waits for a nod before continuing. "That won't do. She wants freedom, her only limits are the ocean and the horizon. Last time I found her in Aesheim and had to drag her halfway across the known world. She wants freedom, therefore the wards are her most significant obstacle because she can't leave the city until they're inverted or destroyed."

Realisation dawns on Andrian's face and he pulls a face. "The ward hub."

"Oh good, bureaucracy hasn't killed your critical thinking skills, there's a good Seeker Seer," Lark says with a smirk. "I always wondered."

"She could be there already!"

"Oh, I'd be *astounded* if she isn't," Lark says, and it takes a moment for reality to crash through the high of proving their own cleverness. It is an ugly, brutal moment that wrenches the air from their lungs. "Scholar's mind, we need to go. No time to waste. Nice to meet you, Cillian!"

Lark grabs Wren's hand and sprints from the building in the hope that the adrenaline will battle the guilt and accusation of stupidity in their chest.

"Best of luck!" Cillian calls after them. "Try not to die!"

Adrenaline wins the battle. Instead of wondering what they will find at their destination, Lark focuses on the journey. Having spent several years of university in the holy city and then many return visits since graduation, Lark has almost every street memorised. The ward hub is ten minutes at a breakneck run and they waste no time or breath. Every turn is half instinct.

And then — they are there, the distinctive structure in sight. Spires protrude from the roof, topped with small orbs, transmitters that pair with the border wards and keep the security system protected.

A figure is slumped against the wall. Unmoving and bent uncomfortably. Wren moves to investigate, but is stopped by Lark's hand and a solemn shake of their head. She blinks, then steels her expression and follows their direction without argument.

Adrenaline is no longer winning. Lark wills their body to be calm, their mind to not race ahead. One step at a time.

The pair head further in. Through another door that hangs off its hinges, a chain of keys lies discarded on the floor. There is another body. No marks. The usual.

The ward hub is accessed by this singular entryway, a walkway carrying those who enter above the cavern that is lined with rune engraved stone. Symbols glimmer with magic as blue as the dome they had seen above the city.

The room hums with energy, the vibrations of magic in a concentrated form, a comforting rhythm. Another sound is interrupting it, the erratic scratching of a quill on paper. Lark's stomach turns.

Closer. They creep around the central column of the hub. Another still body is sprawled across the metal grate floor. This one drips with blood from the fingertips, neck, and orifices.

And past it... *her*.

A waterfall of auburn curls down her back, her dark coat that falls to mid thigh — filthy with several years of prison muck, skin past pale to the point of sickly. Knee high boots, sturdy and practical. There is a reek of damp, of must and darkness and seclusion.

"Lark," she says without even turning around, "you took longer than I thought."

Chapter 3

LARK HAS SPENT MANY rogue moments, many midnight hours, and countless forbidden allotments of time imagining what it might be like to see Nightingale again. What it might feel like to hear their name roll off her tongue, soft and tender and like a kiss in the dark.

The reality is visceral; a chill rolls down their spine, trembles their entire body every inch of the way, and it is apprehension and desire and a battle for restraint all at once. Their stomach is meanwhile choosing violence.

They try to speak her name but cannot — she hasn't turned around. The magic instilled in Lark's being demands a strict protocol and will not release their voice until it is followed. A little choked noise comes out instead.

"Oh, darling, I'm sorry. I forgot."

Nightingale turns. Violet eyes, rimmed in large round glasses, meet Lark's and light for a moment like the pulse of an amethyst. Then her gaze flicks to Wren and narrows, the light dying as her lips purse.

Her right hand begins scribbling in the notebook she has strapped to her right thigh, face up. *How many has she gone through?*

Naturally, now that Lark *can* speak to her, their mind conjures no words whatsoever.

"How have you been?" they ask, without meaning to.

Nightingale laughs. "Oh. You know. Incarcerated. Thank you ever so much, darling." The sass slides from her face and voice as she adds, "Thank you for the notebooks. Truly."

"Of course. I wasn't sure how much you would need them, but I know you can't—"

"Guards talk. I filled four." Her eyes flick to Wren and she smiles, prettily, like a venomous snake. "Introduce us?"

"Oh!" Lark claps their hands together. "Yes yes yes, Nightingale, this is Wren." They glance at Wren and gesture wildly. "Wren, Nightingale."

Wren has perfected a new art of expressing bafflement with impeccable rigidness of body. As Nightingale waves with a waggle of fingers and a disturbing giggle, Wren gives a polite nod in return.

"So, it's official, then, that you like redheads?" Nightingale asks with a smirk.

As Wren's pale cheeks glow pink, Lark sighs. There is genuine, threatening curiosity veiled in the question, paired with burning in Nightingale's eyes of *who is she to you? Is she what I was?*

As if anyone, ever, could be anything close.

"Wren is a friend," they say.

"How nice," Nightingale says, and Lark hears it as *how nice that she can continue breathing.* "So, tea? Dinner? A night on the town?"

Down to unfortunate business then.

"You need to come back, Nightingale," Lark says, because they need to, because useless words are better than not trying at all.

"What, because you still think that this," Nightingale gestures to the body at her feet with free hand, "is a problem?"

"Killing people for your own greed? Yes."

"I was hoping you'd change your tune back to something we could sing together," Nightingale says, sighing.

"You know I don't sing."

Nightingale clicks her tongue. "And you know that isn't what I mean. Will it be a dance, then? Will you be able to—"

A flare of bright orange magic slams Nightingale in the side.

Hanging from the metal walkway, pulling themself up with trembling arms, is a magical technician dressed in robes of The First Inventor, the Autumn goddess. They are blonde, bloodied, and shaking.

"Oh," Nightingale says, sounding put out. "Didn't I kill you already?"

"No," the technician says with gritted teeth, "you threw me over the side."

"Oh yes, because you were in my way and boring me. I remember." Nightingale smiles and it turns Lark's blood cold. "Shall we rectify my mistake?"

With a flash of purple magic, Nightingale is gone and appears right behind the technician, seizing them in a hold from behind that keeps their arms locked in place. A quick wave from her occupied hand and she pulls them both back through the portal that appears.

Lark cannot move fast enough to follow. Wren is frozen, and probably best so. Above them, the scream of the technician echoes through the chamber, an awful rattling cry as they dangle from Nightingale's arm.

Nightingale laughs, holding onto a groove in the central arcane capacitor with a tight grip. Something swings from her neck, a porcelain mask on a chain.

"Now, here's the thing, honey," she says to the technician, "arm strength? Not my best point. So how long do you think you've got before I drop you?"

"Why are you doing this?" the technician screams.

"Because four walls for three years is *so* dull. You can't begin to imagine." Nightingale groans a moment later, the strain of holding the technician's weight now showing through the red flush across her skin, the tension in her jaw. "Oof. Not long now. Good try, kid."

The technician's eyes find Lark's, swimming in confusion and desperation. Lark scrambles for a solution, for anything at all, while Wren starts climbing the central pillar.

Nightingale's hand opens. The technician falls. Lark runs, arms outstretched. It isn't enough. Lark squeezes their eyes shut.

"You're..." Wren does not seem to find a word that conveys the magnitude of the horror of it all.

A crackle of magic puts Nightingale right next to Wren just as Lark opens their eyes again.

"Finish that sentence, flowers," Nightingale dares, voice low and lethal. "See what happens."

"You don't care what I think."

"No, I don't. But I still have my pride. And I still have them."

Nightingale and Wren look at Lark in the same instant, and Lark fails them both by finding they have no response at all.

Nightingale rolls her eyes. "Bored now."

"I'm so *sorry*," Wren says, swinging her sword at Nightingale's knees and forcing her to leap backward. "Let's fix that."

"Ooh, she's got some spirit, she's got some spirit, nice," Nightingale says, grinning. "But can she *run*?"

"I'm not running from you."

"Hm. Didn't think you liked them stupid, darling," Nightingale says to Lark, "but if you want her alive, I'd get going."

Wren's sword swings again. Nightingale, prepared, steps through a portal and appears on the other side of a column.

"Oh, teleport magic is *cheating*," Wren mutters.

"This many square feet of enchanted runes, what kind of explosion do you think that makes?" Nightingale asks Lark. "I think I'll find out. Stay and see if you like, but you might get a bit... decimated."

"Nightingale," Lark says, pained and horrified, cursing how they are still able to be shocked by the depths she will sink to. "Please. No."

Nightingale smiles. Her next words are soft. "Say it again."

Lark swallows. They close their eyes just for a moment. "Please."

The moments spent locked in her gaze could be hours. There is a shine to her violet eyes, a curl to her lips that reminds them of when she would find a particularly beautiful line of poetry and for a moment relish it all on her own before sharing it with them.

And then —

"No."

The moment is obliterated by a word with the force of a warhammer. Nightingale smirks, slips the porcelain mask onto her face, and begins to utter an incantation in a guttural, harsh tongue. Lark still does not know which entity she is calling on. There are words they would exchange if they did. If they could.

Magic crackles and the hub whines in protest. Lark is tugged back, jerked out of the haze of watching Nightingale invoke her magic on a new level.

"Lark," Wren says, pulling them around to face her, the rotation of their whole body effortless for her, "are we getting clear or stopping her? I don't like the sound of this."

"Decisions decisions," Nightingale sing songs unhelpfully from behind them.

Lark stares up at the column and feels the tension in the air, the magic potential of the world itself beginning to bend and twist around the vicinity.

The future forks ahead of Lark. A choice, a question. *If I make this explode, will you try to stop me and risk failing, risk this silly new friend of yours, or will you take the guaranteed outcome?*

It is no choice at all. Risking Wren is not an option.

They grab Wren's hand and pull her into a run with every bit of strength they can muster. The manipulation and stretch of the magic is making the potential within Lark restless and excited, magic reaching for magic, chaos seeking chaos.

Instead of fighting it down, Lark lets it give every stride a boost, riding the surge of extra energy because every foot might be the difference between life or loss of limb. And with it so attuned to every inch of them they can feel when it is going to

—

Lark slams into Wren's side, driving her to dive for cover as much as they are able, and she pulls them forward as they fall. Lark begins to utter a frantic prayer, their hand reaching for their amulet.

Everything around them shatters. The world goes white, and magical force slams them in the back. Deep cracks of fracturing stone echo like a choir as the building comes down. Piece by piece, yet all at once, stone after stone falling all around them.

A sheen of divine energy, just enough to cover Lark and Wren's bodies both, flickers with every hit it takes for them. They are curled together, Wren's larger body covering Lark's while Lark has their eyes squeezed shut as their mouth moves in a circular prayer that can be repeated over and over to sustain the Scholar's magic.

"Scholar, preserve my mind and the body that carries it, preserve what must endure and grow and learn for many more seconds, preserve my heart and essence with the potential borrowed and potential I shall one day return to. I embody you and so protect me, Scholar, preserve my mind and that body that carries it..."

A large chunk of stone thunders above them. The hit to the shield makes Lark gasp and grip the magic tighter.

"You can do this," Wren says to them quietly. "It's almost settled. Keep going."

Lark keeps murmuring their words. The magic itself is taxing but in a way so familiar it is no different than managing other bodily functions. But every spell has its limit.

Eventually, Lark's prayer is the only sound left. They glance around and let the words fall away, with a soft final thank you for the protection.

The shield flickers to nothing. All around them, jagged slabs of stone have encased them in a dusty, cramped prison.

"Should I try to shift some of this?" Wren asks.

Lark considers what they can see, the angles, potential paths of movement. "Carefully. Slowly. Just to see. We need to know how deep we are."

Wren's armour scrapes against stone as she adjusts and the sound makes them both wince. With her legs firmly planted, she gets her arms into position against the stone most prominently above them.

A sweat breaks out across her forehead the moment she pushes. Lark stares up at her with fascination, admiring her strong jaw and absently considering that this would be a different sight altogether if she were wearing a vest instead of full plate armour.

It's funny knowing that so many people lose their minds over muscular people and their biceps and such things. Or people with large bottoms.

Lark had thought for a long time that it was not something they would ever experience — being over twenty years in when many get such feelings in their teens, the logic simply pointed that way. Until one day, years into the friendship with Nightingale, there had been a moment where Lark had glanced over and been caught by the line of her neck where it met her collarbone and wondered what it would taste like.

But it had only ever been her.

Now, watching Wren in the incredible feat of strength as she shifts stone of incredible weight just enough to create a gap above them, Lark stares at the curl of Wren's lips as she smiles at her small victory. She glances at Lark and her cheeks colour at the attention, a gorgeous shade of deeper red against the pink of exertion. Something stirs in Lark's stomach.

The fascinating thing about the world? There are always chances for new things.

It is a relief in more ways than one when they hear grinding and cracks above them. Lark laughs, breathlessly, at the hope of rescue, at the fact that they are once again a survivor of something impossible. One day the audacity of their existence may catch up to them, but not today.

Wren, resting instead of risking injury or disaster, lets out a small laugh that echoes Lark.

"Gods, the Scholar really likes you."

"I know," Lark says with a grin. "Good, isn't it?"

A few more minutes pass and tiny shafts of daylight begin to creep through as the rubble is cleared. Finally, the sky is above them once more and they groan as they get to their feet, stiff from being bent the wrong way too long.

The sun is blocked out by a wide, imposing figure standing at the edge of their little crater.

"Seeker Lark, congrats on not being dead," says a harsh voice as a strong and callused hand reaches out to help them make the final step. "It looks like you need help catching this Nightingale bitch, so the Bishops sent me to assist. I hope you're worth the rescue."

Chapter 4

THE NEW ARRIVAL IS a broad, armoured woman with dwarven blood who looks like she could hold her own against Wren or possibly even *win*. Her dark hair and beard are both braided with beads of many colours throughout, indicating a life filled with biological family and chosen bonds in multitudes.

So, naturally, her face is displaying an incredibly personable scowl.

"Charmed," Lark says brightly, shaking the hand that lifted them free. "What was your name?"

"Ser Palla, of the Temple of War."

Lark has complicated feelings on the Temple of the Warbringer and the people that follow it. Balance is an important aspect of the world, certainly, and the existence of war is part of that balance. All the same, previous experiences leave them apprehensive. Their gaze lingers on the symbol carved into Palla's armour, the golden shield with the red claw marks tearing across it. A large axe is hanging off her belt.

"Fascinating choice of backup on the Bishops' part," Lark says, "but thank you, thank you for the rescue. Remarkable response time. Only a few minutes, to get here and move all this?"

"We'd received a report about a dead body outside the building," Palla says, "and the Bishops had already sent for me. Lucky you."

"It's wonderful to know that you feel as good about this rescue as I do," Lark tells her.

"Hi, Wren, I'm here too," Wren interrupts, as she comes to stand at Lark's side. "Question. If she has teleport magic, how do we catch her?"

"Even she doesn't have unlimited magic, no one does," Lark says. They roll their body to try and appease the protesting muscles. "She's just getting in a head start."

"Quite a big head start," Wren says dubiously.

Palla's scowl deepens. "I'll say."

"Yes, but she can't leave the city until the outer ward projectors run out of their reserves, which will take a day or two. And finding things happens to be one of my specialties — however, is your intention to come with us as we pursue Nightingale?"

Such a casual use of her name on their tongue, in such an essential question, after so long of trying to avoid it.

"Obviously."

"I'm afraid that's not advisable," Lark says, "the Bishops couldn't have anticipated this scale of damage and someone needs to coordinate an emergency repair of the core system. And if you come with us, it sets the wrong precedent for Nightingale."

Palla blinks, her astonishment swirling turquoise around her many braids. "The wrong *precedent*? Are you as mad as they say?"

"You, with Wren and I already in play? She'll perceive it as a true threat."

"Good!"

Lark stands their ground, and cannot help the sneer that turns their mouth. "No, *Ser Palla*, it is not *good*. Right now she is embracing freedom. She will be treating it like a game, but not one she intends to lose, not ever. She just blew up one of the most essential buildings in the city because she was bored and wanted to make a spectacle. Her being loose is bad enough, but may every god help us if she ever actually feels *threatened*. There is a chance, a small chance, that I can apprehend her before she does something beyond her usual atrocities. I have to try."

Palla's skull looks in danger of exploding from the flurry of colours racing across her skin, even more in Lark's vision shifting and battling with a ferocity that her god would be proud of. Her dark eyes flick towards the wreckage of the ward hub.

"You have one hour," she says. "Then I get involved. If you fuck around, those lives are on you."

"I know, I know. Now—"

With a smile, Lark grasps their holy symbol and focuses on what they wish to find. Or rather, who. Nightingale, ever glorious, ever horrendous, smirks in Lark's mind. A quick request of a prayer later, and a strong tug in Lark's gut pulls them southwest.

"This way," they say, looking between Wren and Palla before grabbing Wren's hand. "Ready to run?"

"Always."

The chase well and truly begins. The buildings and people blur as they dash through the streets, following the pull of the magic.

Lark loves to run. Their legs often feel differently on the matter, and their binder is quick to return to its unhelpful habit of keeping full breaths just out of reach. Still, there is nothing to be done about that, since speed and dignity are allergic to the process of binder removal.

Luckily, perseverance and ignoring common sense have seldom led Lark wrong in the past. They push on. Each fevered beat of their heart pushes another frantic stride. Nightingale cannot escape. Too many lives hang in the balance of the moments about to follow.

The bridge to the western side of town is their next way forward. It stretches before them, a splendor of polished cobblestones reflecting the sun off the soft cream — and beyond them, Lark spies a gleam of dark red.

"Sorry, excuse me, coming through," Lark says to anyone they have to push past, the words coming out a bit hoarse.

Wren is hot on their heels, the already astounding athleticism all the more impressive for the speed she can move in her armour.

The dark red curls turn and the cold mask stares back. Nightingale blows a kiss in Lark's direction and teleports again.

The magical bearing Lark has fixed on her shifts so drastically in direction that their stomach turns over and nearly brings up their lunch.

"You alright?" Wren asks.

"Fine," Lark says, skidding to a halt. One second to breathe. Another second to let their stomach settle. Last second for grabbing Wren's firm bicep to bring her with them. "This way. She won't lose us so easily."

The western market is a crowded complication. Had it truly only been perhaps an hour since they had been here, showing Wren their favourite foods and laughing at how she wrinkled her freckled nose at raisin biscuits? It feels like a year.

Nightingale should not have such an impact on their perception of reality. It is mortifying.

The woman in question is across the way, dozens of people between them unknowingly serving as effective obstacles. She reaches into a crate on the edge of a stall and takes something out.

She has the nerve to lower the mask and catch Lark's eye as she does it, pocketing it with one of those smirks that sends Lark's body into an uproar. Then — another teleport. Another stomach churning shift in the bearing. Lark ignores it and hurries to examine the crate in question, Wren at their back.

"Apples?!" Lark cries, with bewilderment. "How can it be *apples*? What she grabbed was smaller, I know it."

The stall owner, a tall horned man with skin as golden as coins, lifts an eyebrow at them. "Nothing in there but apples, friend. I would know. They're mine."

"Fine, fine, apples apples apples, make it make *sense*," Lark mutters to themself.

The aura around the merchant is a distinct mix of confusion and curiosity. A convincing asset in their argument, certainly, but —

"Lark, she's getting away," Wren tells them, putting a hand on their shoulder.

Lark wordlessly points in the new bearing direction. Wren takes off without another word. Lark takes several moments to breathe as deeply as they can, cursing the constriction that usually brings euphoria more than anything. If they had just known what this day would bring...

Such a silly little thing, when Wren is going full speed with armour and no sign of faltering. Training the body can truly pay off as much as training the mind. Who knew?

Onward. Pushing through it all, praying to the Scholar for mercy on the weakness of their body — it is all in the service of goodness and knowledge and learning. Nightingale is nowhere in sight but Wren is well ahead and following the small changes in bearing without direction from Lark. *Line of sight. Good.*

Their path is taking them over another bridge, back to the eastern side. Nightingale is halfway across, with Wren just reaching the start. The former teleports to the next bridge over, one hundred feet south. Wren does not hesitate and merely runs faster, disappearing around a corner.

Lark is halfway over the bridge when the bearing on Nightingale vanishes.

They grab their symbol and concentrate once again, reaching into the magical potential of the world around them and seeking Nightingale's essence within it. There is nothing. Nothing at all. As if she doesn't exist.

Chapter 5

To DESCRIBE THE CURRENT situation as being 'blindsided' feels like too drastic of an understatement. Nightingale has vanished from the sight of the Scholar's magic. Now, blocking magic is hardly impossible. But Nightingale has been imprisoned for several years, cut off from everyone. Access to a possible item powerful enough to hide her from Lark's sense is hardly a common prison escape gift in this city. Could it have been what she had grabbed from the crate? Even though the owner of the crate seemed to know nothing?

The theorising is useless. Catching Nightingale is all that matters.

Baffled and panicked, Lark reaches the end of the bridge, eyes searching frantically for the women ahead of them. But Wren is still running. Wren has not even faltered.

"Can you still see her?" Lark shouts as loudly as possible.

"She's not so fast," Wren calls back, with a smug grin.

"We can't lose her, or countless people could be hurt! I can't trace her, but perhaps if you stay on her I can find a place to cut her off."

Wren has the sense to look alarmed at the mention of the trace not working, and to not ask further questions. She pushes further forward after the matchstick form of Nightingale along the road. Lark, hoping to everything that they get lucky, makes a sharp left turn and heads north. Stray, frantic thoughts bombard Lark with every slap of their boots against the paved streets.

Once Lark swats them away, horror seeps in to take their place. They have sent Wren after Nightingale, alone. Nightingale could kill Wren as easily as any of the guards at the ward battery. Wren's skill is near inconsequential in the face of Nightingale's magic and amorality.

Emotions are such messy things. Lark stops to catch their breath, and wills themself against getting lost in a spiral of violent and upsetting hypotheticals. *Get it together, for the Scholar's sake,* they tell their lungs. Gasping at air is so undignified and counterproductive.

A flash of red. Nightingale. Entering the northeastern sector from the south, crossing it to continue north. Lark's mind races, tracing their mental map of the city, committed to memory long ago. What could she possibly be headed for? North only holds...

The university. The place that holds the kind of power she would need to *stay* ahead of Lark, once out of the city.

"I'm such an idiot," Lark mutters. They cast a look back, trying to seek Wren's tall strawberry head among the southern streets and crowds, but there is nothing.

Wren. Nightingale. Friend in danger, enemy on the loose. The worst kind of choice. But if Wren were here, her answer would be absolute and unwavering. So Lark pushes down nausea at the thought of Wren dead in an alleyway at Nightingale's hands, and heads north.

The huge building is grandiose and pompous and glorious and Lark never tires of the sight of it, never stops adoring it and all it represents.

There is, however, dissonance everywhere in running into the university after Nightingale, their heart pounding. For a moment it is years before and she is only twenty feet ahead, looking back over her shoulder with mirth and fondness not yet tainted.

"Come on! We're going to be late!" she had shouted.

"Stopping for snacks was your idea!"

"But you're the one who can't keep up!"

Lark is not one for hatred. But there is a small, ugly inch of their heart that desperately wishes to come face to face with whatever entity Nightingale found in her research and reached out to, the one that pushed her into everything that came to tear the two of them apart. More than anything, they simply want to ask if any part of them cares what it is they ruined.

Lark passes the threshold of the building entrance and skids to a halt. Getting their bearings and breath back, Lark closes their eyes for a moment before opening again with focus on the magic that tingles in their left eye. The students in the corridors light like lanterns in a festival. Many hues of blue, different trails of thoughtfulness and curiosity, plenty of yellow and orange for happiness and excitement. Turquoise in tiny spots where students are stuck on things. That's closer to what Lark is looking for — the turquoise mingled with grey and pale yellow. It's there, a small ripple of confusion and worry riding the shouts of alarm down the corridor.

"There you are," Lark murmurs.

A tap on their shoulder. They whirl around, heart leaping out of their ribcage. Wren's green eyes and freckles fill Lark's vision.

"That was fast," they say, agape.

Wren shrugs and gestures to the left side of Lark's face, where emerald and gold scales mix around the draconic eye. "You're easy to follow. People notice you. She's here, then?"

"That way," Lark says, pointing down the corridor while their eyes remain fixed on Wren. Their feet itch to move, their gaze to chase Nightingale's path. But they cannot, not until they are finished speaking. "Caution, Wren, she is—"

"Unpredictable and dangerous?" Wren asks, beginning to walk in the direction they had pointed. "That's obvious enough. And soon, you can explain why you talk to her like you do."

Lark wants to say that there is nothing to discuss. The words refuse to leave their mouth, because Wren is ahead of them, her face turned away. They can only run to catch up and meanwhile curse the magical phenomenon that has plagued them since the day it all went wrong.

The colourful auras of the students lead them up several flights of stairs and into the faculty offices. With each turn of the corridors a new thread of theory weaves into shape in Lark's mind. The shape is a worrying one.

A door forced off its hinges awaits them. It belongs to an office that Lark knows all too well.

"I was right," they say when they come to a stop outside and are able to look at Wren. "She wants to get away. It's lucky Professor Amaya wasn't in here when she was."

"And you know this because..."

"Look at the cabinet."

Wren frowns and steps into the office. Her eyebrows crease into a frown as she regards the shelves lined with round, golden devices that resemble a compass but are engraved with runes all around the circumferences, solid enough to require two hands to hold steady. Glass lies in fragments at the base of the cabinet and one of the stands is empty.

"Wayfinders," Wren says, amazed. "I know you told me yours wasn't the only one, but—"

"But they are exceedingly rare, and seldom awarded," Lark says with a nod. They step into the room. "I was actually awarded mine for capturing Nightingale. Our history was well known and I was commended for putting the safety of our country's citizens and reputation ahead of my personal feelings."

"So now she's taken one of her own," Wren says, with a twist at the edge of her mouth. "Fitting, really." She glances at Lark. "That must have been complicated for you."

"Everything is a complicated day, when Nightingale is involved." Lark sighs. Wren's body is bathed in dark blue curiosity and pale yellow concern and Lark must ignore both. They turn their eyes to the cabinet and the ostentatious gap instead. Then, after a moment's consideration, back to

Wren. "The thing is, you can't just *take* a Wayfinder. There is an attunement ritual, initiated only by the High Bishop himself—"

Lark stops dead. And bolts out the door.

"Lark!"

Wren follows after her shout, which goes unanswered because it must. Two paths in the university lead to the Temple of the Scholar — the ground floor thoroughfare and the faculty suites. And in that temple... is the one person who can give Nightingale the final key to her freedom.

Lark might not be able to track Nightingale anymore, but the High Bishop is a simple matter and Lark is pulled in a straight shot west through the building, as they knew they would be.

"Lark!" Wren calls as she catches up. "Damnit! Explain! Please!"

Lark skids to a stop at a railing on the edge of some stairs. One way goes down to the thoroughfare, the other continues on through the offices. Lark turns to look at Wren.

"We can't do that *and* chase her, Wren, it's talk or run! She's already got a headstart—"

"Look, I've never brought up your weird thing about eye contact in conversation before. But this is ridiculous."

"Wren, I *can't*," Lark says, a part of them screaming as it has for several years in protest at the absurdity of it all. The indignity. The impracticality. "It's not a choice. I physically cannot speak a single word to someone without looking them in the eyes. I try. The words won't come out. It's like... a curse. Four years now. Every waking moment."

The bafflement on Wren's face would be portrait worthy in any other moment. "That's the most ridiculous thing I've ever heard," Wren says, attempting to laugh. It's hollow.

"Try living it!" Lark's hands gesture frantically. "Wren, she's getting away. The High Bishop is in danger. Please. I will answer your questions once we have her."

"Fine, come on," Wren says. She grabs their arm and pulls them back into a sprint, around the landing to the door on the other side. "Is this the way?"

Lark nods and they start up again. It's liberating, to have explained the magical block to Wren. How it came about is another matter entirely, of course, as is Nightingale's side of things. But Lark has promised an explanation and they *will* give it. Soon.

With that weight off, the adrenaline of running at top speed through a place that had once been their whole world, and the binder refusing passage to a single full breath, Lark's head is spinning.

The door at the seam of the buildings is grand, polished wood and is ajar when it should be locked. Lark swallows and pushes it open as quietly as possible so that they and Wren can creep onto the higher balcony of the temple.

The moment they step inside the body of the place, Lark feels a sense of serenity. The gods are strange beings, never speaking to mortals directly, but bestowing their power to the most faithful of their followers. For the followers of the Scholar, they pass through the university first, and at graduation they see if their belief is powerful enough to manifest Gifted magic. Lark's years of devotion and research outshine most. The Scholar's power is at their fingertips to use as they deem fit — more and more every day, a gift in return for their service, their loyalty.

In contrast, the draconic eye twitches in its socket and Lark has to fight a shiver in the same moment. It is almost as if a part of it understands that the magic that restored it to life came from this god, from the essence of this place.

It's long dead, Lark had once said as they turned the rotting flesh over in their hands.

So bring it back, Nightingale had countered, *you've regrown arms. What is one eye? Are you so afraid of dragon magic?*

The challenge had been too immense, too impossible to turn down. And once complete, the power too tempting to not seize.

It is a weakness the two of them share, now and forever.

Lark can see Nightingale crouched in the sanctuary, leaning over the still form of the High Bishop, her hand gripping his forehead.

"Shit," Wren whispers from beside them, "I'm so sorry, if I hadn't—"

Lark puts their hand over hers where it sits on the bannister. "He's been dead a little while now. She's extracting."

"What?"

"She doesn't kill for no reason, Wren," Lark says, keeping their voice to a whisper so it does not echo in the huge space. "She kills because she can extract secrets from corpses. Either something specific she wants to know, or a secret only that person knew. She wants to know everything, always has."

"You want to know everything," Wren counters, "and you don't—"

"I thank the Scholar every day that I did not receive power that would tempt me into something so horrible, because I don't want to assume to be above any temptation," Lark says, forcing themself to be calm. "Come. We need to get down there before she finds what she's after."

The side stairs take them to the ground floor. Just as they step into the main body of the temple, Nightingale's eyes — fixed on the stair exit, waiting — narrow. Her hand rescinds from the robed body of the bishop as annoyance crosses her face for all but a brief scarlet moment. With a flash of magic, she vanishes to a point behind the altar and gives a small wave as her other pulls on her mask.

Lark is running. Lark is shouting her name. And she is there one moment and gone the next in a flash.

It is impossible to turn one's head in as many directions as Lark needs to scour now. Every corner of the temple, every doorway and balcony... nothing.

"I—" Their right hand runs through their hair, the left meanwhile gesturing fruitlessly as they turn to look at Wren. "I don't see her. But she had to have been in *sight*—"

"She must have found a *very* good spot."

"She can't teleport to somewhere she can't see—"

"Good to know, but it must have been somewhere she could see that we couldn't."

A new voice joins theirs, timid and distant. "Is she gone?"

For the first time, Lark takes notice of the civilians huddled in the corners of the temple. Some are inching towards the doors. All are stark and staring, many shaking. Lark wants to comfort them, to offer them reassurance, but every nerve in their body feels like a magical layline.

"She's gone, and you're all safe for now, but I need you to get me Deputy Bishop Andrian," Lark tells the person who had inquired after Nightingale. "Tell him we need a high priority resurrection here, now, and that Nightingale is in the wind. I'll prepare the rite until he arrives."

Chapter 6

ONCE THE OMINOUS MESSAGE is gone and on its way, things get quiet.

Wren, ever wonderful, moves through the sea of civilians and suggests that everyone go home if possible. It is the sort of calm and gentle that Lark could never hope to emulate.

Lark meanwhile gets to work. Moving to the back of the sanctuary, they stare up at the statue of the Scholar looking out over the church, a focused gaze on a clean shaven masculine face. One hand clasps a book and quill close to his chest while the other hand extends a scroll, an offering to join in the learning.

"Forgive the intrusion," Lark says softly, a little smile on their lips.

They swipe a few bottles of blessed oil and water and take it to the High Bishop's side. Prayers then fall from their lips, committed to memory and flowing easily. Their fingers anoint the Bishop in the key areas: the forehead, the temples, the heart, the hands, and the eyelids.

Lark is almost finished when the sound of Andrian's anxiety weighted voice and the clanking of armour interrupt the near silence.

"Lark! Is it — oh, by the Scholar himself."

Lark finishes the preparation rite and sits back on their heels. Only now do they see that the civilians have left and that Wren is sitting on a bench nearby.

Someone is with Andrian — a rather disgruntled Ser Palla. Her horror matches Andrian's but has a distinct flavour of contempt that his lacks.

"He's ready," Lark says.

"Good, another Bishop is on their way to perform the ritual."

"Good, good." Lark's hands twist in front of them. "Andrian, she was here and *vanished*. I can't make sense of it. We *saw* her."

"You were so sure you didn't need my help," Palla says, crossing her arms, "and she's still at large." Her eyes move to the altar. "Could she have used the emergency passage? The Bishop would have had the key on him."

Lark blinks. "What emergency passage?"

Palla's face is dangerously still. "You've got to be kidding." She holds out her hand to Andrian. "Deputy. Your key. Please."

Andrian hands the small key over without a word. Palla takes it into the sanctuary, reaching a hand under the altar for several moments. There is an almost imperceptible click and Lark dashes to watch as a panel of stone slides away to reveal a narrow passage heading down into the earth, an iron ladder lining the way.

"How did I not know about this?!" Lark asks with bemusement. "I'm a Seeker, how does a knight of *another god* know about an emergency exit in *our* temple—"

"It's the same in every temple, brainiac," Palla tells them with a roll of her eyes. "The High Bishop and Deputy of each temple all possess the key to their own."

"Andrian, why did you never—"

Andrian coughs. "Unless I have my history wrong, Lark, you've never held a bishop position," he says wryly. "It would lose its security value if everyone knew about it."

"But *she* knows—"

"Ser Palla is the council's chosen, the destined of the Ascension project, her safety is *more* paramount than any bishop's, of course she knows. Now, are you going to continue to whine or may we—"

"The *Ascension* project?" Lark blinks. "Is *that* what the bishops are cooking up to turn the tide of the war? What is it? Fascinating implications from the name alone—"

"What it is, is need to know," Palla says, voice as gentle as an anvil to the head. "And you do not need to know."

"Indeed," Andrian agrees before Lark can do anything but pout, "but what we *must* know is if the High Bishop's key is missing. Was this Nightingale's point of exit or not?"

Wren is already kneeling by the body and patting the robes down. "I was wondering that too. There's no key I can find."

Lark swallows their pride and curiosity, unpalatable and sour as they are, and fixes their gaze on Palla. "Could you take us to where the passage comes out? I take it you know?"

Palla nods, quiet satisfaction in her eyes. "Of course. Follow me. We've wasted enough time."

The last comment is pointed and would sting most people. Lark is decidedly not most people but can accept that the comment is deserved. They are happy to keep quiet for once and follow Palla out of the temple, Wren falling into step behind them. Andrian, meanwhile, hurries to catch up to Palla and the two begin to talk in hushed tones.

"Are you still thinking about the mysterious project?" Wren asks as they stride through the streets at the fastest sustainable pace.

Lark glances at her, only momentarily alarmed by the accuracy of her guess before they are warmed with affection. It is swallowed a moment later by manic speculation.

"Of course," they say. "*Ascension*. Fascinating word. Endless possibilities. What exactly a whole council of bickering bishops in the middle of a devastating war might have actually agreed on is too terrifying and intriguing to conceive. Especially if they've deemed it not appropriate for public knowledge."

"Let's leave them to that, and focus on Nightingale," Wren suggests. When Lark makes a face, Wren gives them a sympathetic look. "Or are you trying *not* to focus on Nightingale?"

"I don't see why I can't give my mind a break from her until we're closer," Lark says, petulant in their exhaustion, both physical and emotional. "She's a very specific sort of headache."

"When we have more than a few minutes to talk, I have questions about her, just so you know," Wren says. "About what she is to you. If we catch her, it might not be important anymore. But it feels like it'll still be important to you. And you're my friend. If she's a burden, I want to understand."

Lark swallows. "We'll see, Wren. We'll see."

The rest of the trek across the city is silent until Palla comes to a stop.

"That alley there," she says, pointing her gauntleted hand. "So... somewhere in this area."

"Lark? Which way?" Andrian asks.

"I don't know," Lark admits. "My trace isn't working. She's gotten something to block me. I don't know how."

"Oh. That is... very troubling."

"Old fashioned way, then," Palla announces, "come on."

They split into pairs to divide authority and muscle evenly — Palla with Lark, and Wren with Andrian.

It feels wrong, to be barging into people's houses, searching every possible hiding spot. It is a specific sort of cowardice that has Lark hiding behind Palla's status and procedure. Luckily, every citizen regards Palla with awe and there is no resistance.

There is also no Nightingale. Impatience sits heavy in Lark's gut, urging them and taunting them to break away and try something reckless on their own. They might have listened to it if not for a shout down the street about half an hour into the process.

"The Deputy," Palla says at the same time that Lark says, "Wren."

They run at top speed, hearing continued shouts and shuffles from a house nearby. The pair burst in, with Lark murmuring a prayer to the Scholar and summoning divine light to their hands — ready to illuminate or threaten, whatever is needed.

Wren is caught in a grapple with a surprisingly muscular older gentleman who is clothed in a grey dressing gown and utter outrage.

"Sir, I am very sorry," Wren is saying to him, as sincere as anything. "I didn't know. It was just meant to be a joke about a pet to make the situation less awkward."

"That's my *wife*!" the man shouts. "My *cursed wife!* How could a joke about that make the situation less awkward?!"

"Yes, but... how could I know? She's a goldfish! Or looks like one—"

This is, in fact, not the correct thing to say as the man roars with deeper fury and headbutts Wren with a force that has them both groaning and reeling. Lark drops their magic, now less alarmed but staring with bewilderment.

"Alright," Palla says the moment the old man goes for a right hook in Wren's direction. She strides in and picks him up by his scruff even though he is taller than her, "that is enough. Wren, remove yourself before you make the situation worse." She glares at the old man as Wren slips out of the building. "You. Desist in attacking officials of the church state or their freelance assistants. I am sorry for your wife. Are you on a curse removal waiting list?"

"Yes," he mutters, "but it takes time and money, as I'm sure you well know—"

Palla pulls a small notebook from her pocket and scribbles a few things down. "Your fighting spirit is commendable. I'll see you prioritised at the temple of War. Take her there tomorrow."

The man melts into a puddle of gratitude. "Oh, thank you, Ser—"

Lark backs out of the house, seeing no good they can do by remaining.

Wren is staring at the stone of a nearby house with an intensity that gives the impression she is debating if she could beat it in a headbutting competition. Lark approaches and puts their hand on her arm, waiting until she glances their way.

"Are you alright?" they ask.

"Why is everything that has happened to me since I met you so *bizarre*?"

"... magnetism?"

"For you and absurdity? That would explain a bit."

Palla stops back outside just as Andrian comes around the corner, late to the party and requesting answers. Palla gets them all back in their pairs, continuing the work, and Lark is left to relay the strange scene to Andrian. He, perhaps sensibly, only blinks and moves on with his life.

The process is slow. Lark sincerely doubts that Nightingale will be holed up somewhere easy to find, but she needs time to attune her subconscious to the Wayfinder. In short, she needs to sleep.

Perhaps, just one time in their life, Lark will get lucky in something that isn't reckless survival.

A few houses into their next batch, they get a surprise.

"Cillian," Palla says, "I didn't realise you lived in this area."

Cillian, having just opened the door for them with a pleasant greeting, blinks. "Ser Palla," he says, "a surprise to see you at this hour. And with the eccentric Seeker, no less."

"We're searching every house. May we come in?"

"Of course, of course." Cillian steps aside to let them in. They give a smile and a dramatic sweep of the hand. "For Nightingale, I assume? Would screams of agony not usually give away her position?"

"She's smarter than that," Lark says, with more bite to their voice than intended. "She's no mindless killer."

"No, she's your *ex*," Cillian says as they move to pour tea into three cups. Their eyes are bright and excited. "I am so curious about that. No one actually seems to know what happened, just that one day she started murdering people and plucking information right from their *souls* as if they were almanacs—"

A heavy boot slams the ground. "Is this a joke, to you?" Palla asks with a scowl.

Cillian shrinks about three inches and dips his head. "No, Ser. Apologies. We admins are such terrible gossips and it has been such an awful day, I'm trying to make sense of it all." Their tongue wets their lips. "We lost good people today. Any sense is better than nothing."

"I don't think you'll find your sense in bloody history, Cillian," Palla says, "so use your brain and consider it is probably not the Seeker's favourite subject. Have some delicacy."

Cillian's aura shows that his curiosity has barely dampened from the reprimand. It is, however, actions that count — they mumble an apology and don't say another word.

As Palla and Lark move through the rooms of the house to continue their sweep, Lark takes the chance to give Palla a look of intense gratitude.

"Don't mistake this," Palla says when she catches it. "If she gets away because of any misplaced remaining feelings of yours, it's on *you*. No one can afford that. But that doesn't mean I can't realise it must be hard for you."

Lark is ready to say thank you when she turns away. The words stay lodged in Lark's throat as Palla moves back into the hallway and they have no choice but to swallow and stay on her heels.

A hallway cupboard is not the thing that Lark would expect to catch Palla's attention. But the woman stops, squints, and yanks the door open to reveal a descending staircase instead of storage.

Lark's pride is protesting being shown up by Palla twice in one day.

"What's this, Cillian?" Palla calls. "Wine cellar?"

"Not quite." There is a chuckle from the kitchen. "Would you like to see?"

Cillian appears before they can answer, a gliding grace with every movement, and slips between them like liquid. He leads them down the steps.

Lark's entire body goes cold the moment they pass the threshold.

"Strange, isn't it?" Cillian asks as they look back at Lark with amusement. "Or, so I hear from any powerful mage such as yourself who has stepped in. Magic proof basement. I even had an Innate caster in here once — they nearly turned blue. Always good to know the lining still works."

"This would cost a small fortune," Palla says, glancing around. "Why get it?"

"Because if a dragon gets through those wards, I want a good hiding spot. I can't spend my life savings if I'm not *alive.*"

Lark regards the stocked room. One comfortable bed, creased but unoccupied. A full bookshelf. Stocks of preserves. Their eye is uncomfortable and erratic — darting around between Palla, Cillian, and several other places.

So cut off from the Scholar in this place, Lark cannot summon any magic to calm it or themself.

"This place is giving me a dragon sized headache," they mutter as they hurry up the stairs.

Once in the hallway, the sense of warmth, of magic, returns. Lark nearly gasps from the relief of it. The dragon eye settles.

It takes a few more minutes for Palla and Cillian to come back upstairs.

"It's just a pleasure to have been able to help someone *so* esteemed," Cillian is saying to Palla. "The plans they have for you... if even a whisper of what I've heard is true—"

"You should forget about things that aren't yours to take care of," Palla says frankly. "You handle chaos well. Stick to that."

"But for one, shining moment you may be the most important person in all of history," he continues. "I hope I have the privilege of basking in it."

The silence that follows is jagged and dangerous. Palla's dark eyes have the smallest glimmer of hesitation, of indecision. Her hand twitches towards her axe. A moment later she mutters a farewell and leaves the house.

Lark follows her to the door, but once she is gone they cannot resist glancing over their shoulder at Cillian. "Do you know what the *Ascension* project is?"

Cillian is quiet and pensive — but their eyes are still bright. "I hear many interesting things, Seeker. It is hard to say what is true, and what is gossip, from other pencil pushers such as myself. But I think it is safe to say that the Bishops have decided our salvation rests with her. And, perhaps, what they could *do* with her."

"What they could *do* with her?" Lark asks. "What does that mean?"

Cillian shrugs. "Andrian may be more willing to divulge information to you, than to I."

"I see. Thank you. Goodnight."

Lark, body still reeling from the shock of the magic-proof bunker but mind racing, steps out into the warm air. The sky is painted with pastels as the night draws in. Wren is caught, staring at the sight with shining eyes, while Andrian is scribbling furiously on his clipboard to keep with the oral report Palla is delivering.

"I take it you two haven't had any luck either," Lark says.

"Nope," Wren replies, shoulders deflating, visible even under her pauldrons. "She's underground for real. But not in the bunker you two just found? Weird. Talk about paranoid."

"In the face of dragons?" Andrian counters. "Is anything too paranoid? We'd make a bunker for the entire city if enchanting it wouldn't take a decade."

Palla's face is doing a marvellous impression of a block of unforgiving timber. "What now? We have no leads."

"She won't be going anywhere tonight," Lark says. "She needs a whole evening, a proper sleep to attune to the Wayfinder."

"What does that mean?" Wren asks.

"Some magic is too complicated to use immediately — the Wayfinder must be intimately aligned with the mind that taps into it, to have any chance of success. You've seen how unpredictable it can be even with that alignment."

"Indeed. However, when she resurfaces she'll be rested and ready to push us to our limits," Andrian says, "so I suggest you all do the same. Sleep in watches just in case."

"I don't need to rest," Palla says, "I'll organise squadrons of guards at each city gate, so that when she tries to escape in the morning, we're ready for her."

"Excellent idea."

Lark searches through their memory, poring over its pages like a library catalogue until they find the section on area maps. Specifically, this area. "There's an empty house down the next street with a decent second story view. We could hole up in there for the night, Wren."

Wren nods. "Sounds good."

Chapter 7

THEY BID THE OTHERS goodbye and make their way around the corner. The walk to the house, and up the interior stairs, is quiet. Lark had searched it with Palla and found nothing, but the abandoned master bedroom has a dusty bed and large window overlooking the neighbourhood.

Wren begins the lengthy process of taking off her armour, and Lark moves to help out of habit. It is a ritual cultivated in their travels. There is a pleasantness about the silent cooperation in such close quarters, about the tiny butterflies in Lark's stomach when Wren's hand brushes theirs on the way to the next plate. Lark cannot, will not, place those butterflies as anything more than a funny and fanciful feeling. Even so, that does not detract from the joy of them.

"Lark," Wren says, voice soft.

Lark looks up and is lost in gentle green eyes. Their hands still. "Yes? Wren?" Their heart pounds in anticipation, for fear of questions they do not want, for fear that it may be something else altogether.

"How are you? Really?"

The sigh that leaves them is exhaustion given breath. "Wren..." they say, "it is so, awfully, terribly complicated."

"Because you loved her?" Wren asks. Lark frowns at her, and she hurries to add, "Andrian mentioned. He wants to help you. He sees how hard it is."

"Yes, yes, everyone is feeling incredibly and uselessly sympathetic today," Lark retorts, letting go of Wren's armour and walking backward to sit on the bed. "If he really knew, he wouldn't be using past tense. But this is Andrian. He has the emotional breadth of a thimble."

"So you still love her, then? Even with everything she's done, everything she's doing?" Wren's tone is neutral, but the words are accusing. Lark cannot help how their gut twists.

"Have you ever been in love, Wren?" Lark asks. "Ever found someone that made you a better version of yourself, made you feel like you would never be alone or truly lost in despair again in your life, so long as they were by your side?"

Wren swallows. Her silence says more than any words could. She has never come close. She is shrouded in soft blue.

"That kind of connection, that kind of meeting of minds and hearts is not so easily discarded," Lark says, "My heart is a traitor to the world but true to itself. I am its warden as I am hers."

The indigo of heartbreak swims around Wren's head. "Lark, that's–"

"I am doing everything in my power to ensure that my past with her is an asset and not a detriment. She is so much more dangerous than even Andrian can comprehend, her perception of the world more advanced... it has to be me. Every time."

Wren licks her lips. "That doesn't seem fair on you."

"Life isn't fair, Wren," Lark mutters, with a rare touch of bitterness.

"What actually *happened* to her?"

Lark laughs, feeling an odd, hollow feeling creep across their chest. A deep breath in. Then out. *She can be trusted,* they tell themself. "That's the thing, Wren. That's what none of them know. It happened to *both* of us."

"What do you mean?"

"Her research led her to... unconventional areas. She acted as though she was still beholden to the Scholar, but I found out later that she stumbled across someone — or something — that offered her more. Powerful magic and knowledge beyond her wildest dreams. The knowledge, at least, she was eager to share with me. She told me she'd learned of a place, of a relic within, so old and powerful it would be the discovery of a lifetime."

Lark stops and swallows. Wren's gaze is intent, her armour now off and set aside, as she comes to kneel in front of them to put them on even standing.

The memories burn as the words spill out, but with each one that is released, Lark feels lighter.

"She was right about that part, at least," they say, choking on another laugh that is not right at all. "We found it, this orb of *something*, abandoned but pulsing, in some structure of the old elves so ancient it would take years to decipher the depictions."

"And then?"

"Well, it was brimming with magic," Lark whispers, "what do you think we did? We had to see. My magic only goes so far. Some things have to be felt. And... from the moment we laid our hands on it, we have never been the same."

Wren is caught between one breath and the next. She manages to say, "how?"

"I lost the ability to speak to another person without giving them my full attention," Lark says, and Wren's eyes widen with new comprehension, "while she is compelled to write down everything and anything she learns, no matter how small. Hence the notebooks, the constant notebooks. But it was a trade, maybe even a fair one. For the inconvenience, she gained the power to take the secrets of the dead — and I can learn history from the inanimate."

"Gods." Wren's eyebrows crease together a moment later. "You never said that was a magic thing. I just thought you were a history nerd."

"I am," Lark says, smiling. "It's strange. People love to talk about the potential around us, about how magic is either given or borrowed and if you borrow from the potential you must give it back. Like it's living. A fascinating point of study, to be sure, but when my magic was gifted to me, why would I linger on it?"

They lick their lips.

"But... in that moment, I think... it knew us. It knew us, and greeted us, and enhanced us as we were, our existing strengths."

Wren is quiet, awed. Her thoughts turn over visibly.

"I can demonstrate, if you would like to hand over your sword."

Wren fetches it and places it gingerly in Lark's lap. They are grateful; their arms would protest the weight of the two-hander.

Lark runs their hand over the cold steel, over the masterful engravings, finer than thread. They close their eyes and reach within themself for that hunger for knowledge that has defined them and driven them for so long. It sparks with magic instantly and tingles across Lark's hand where it is in contact with the sword.

Images race across Lark's mind's eye. Faces, one resembling Wren, names and whispered words, the heat of a forge and then of a battle. The first time Wren's teenage hands ever took it up.

Lark smiles at Wren as the history concludes.

"Your father made this," they say, "early in his blacksmithing career. When he could find no one suitable to wield it, he took it upon himself to learn. And then he taught you. You've been using it for nearly eight years."

Wren, who had only ever referred to it as her father's sword, with no further detail, gapes in an endearingly unbecoming manner.

Lark has to laugh. "Nice little trick, isn't it? I have a funny theory. Would you like to hear it?"

"Sure." Wren takes the sword and props it back up next to her backpack. She sits next to Lark on the bed and they turn to face her, tucking their feet up to sit cross legged.

"Do you remember, about a week after we met, you told me about the band of green stars you could see on the nights of the full moon and the days either side?"

Of all the things she might have expected them to say, this clearly had not been any of them. The puzzlement on her face is so delightful that they wish they could capture it forever somehow; they memorise every line and curve and shine in that moment like it is a page of a book holding something crucial.

"I do," Wren says. "What does that have to do with anything?" She blinks a moment later. "Wait, no, you told me you had seen it for years. But that most people who leave regular life for adventure or magic tend to start seeing it."

Lark nods. "It's true. There's nothing really *written* about it, but if you talk to enough people–"

"Which you do—"

"—which I do, yes," Lark laughs. "But... patterns start to emerge. Almost all of them report a correlation of seeing those stars, and sometimes oddities others cannot, with the emergence of some small boost in their abilities. You told me your swings felt stronger, your understanding of the animals around you deeper, without you having done anything to warrant the change. I remember when a few of my magical abilities took on little quirks. The same."

Wren is pensive. "Why have I never heard about this before?"

"Because I'm not sure how many people actually know about it! They chalk it up to magical anomalies and move on, because it is so subtle. But the more I talked to people, the more it starts to make sense. Mages, especially Innate ones or Disciplined researchers constantly dabbling in new magic, seem to experience this phenomenon earlier in their life than someone such as yourself. But there's also what I didn't tell you that day, Wren."

The wave of doubt that washes over her is a tumultuous swirl of turquoise and grey. She licks her lips. "... alright. And that was..."

Lark swallows. No one but Nightingale knows this, and Lark is not looking to advertise it as a whole, but this is Wren. Besides, one cannot avoid being a magical oddity when they have already replaced their eye with that of a dragon.

"Nightingale and I see those stars *every* night. Ever since that day, since that new power." Lark's hands are moving and gesturing with the force of their enthusiasm. "So it's as if it is the same thing again! But more powerful. Perhaps a higher or deeper threshold that most do not reach, of whatever this is. We did. And it changed everything."

Wren is quiet, eyes thoughtful and careful. "Changed everything because she started killing. Because she could get secrets from her victims. Because she's compelled to get that knowledge?"

"Not compelled to get it, to record it," Lark corrects. "That's the thing. If the compulsion was to seek the knowledge, then this would not strictly be her fault. The compulsions, the blocks, whatever form it takes, it is impossible to bypass. That's why I saw to ensure she had as many notebooks as she needed. But she is not forced to get the information. That is her, purely her, and I could have no part in it. She is so hungry for knowledge, so entitled, that she thinks the lives insignificant compared to what *she* gains."

The silence that follows is so weighted, so agonising, that Lark can only drop their eyes to their hands and run their fingertips over the golden scales scattered across the left wrist.

The sensation is comforting, the way scales can be smooth and rough all at once, direction depending.

Warm, muscular arms encircle Lark's shoulders and pull them close. Lark inhales sharply, not quite expecting it, but then the breath leaves them with a shudder as they fall into the hug with bone deep exhaustion.

"I'm here with you," is all that Wren says, "and I will help however I can. Thank you for trusting me with all this."

Lark's fingers clutch her shirt with a vice grip. It has been so long since they have been held like this, since the loneliness from Nightingale's turn had infected every part of their being and made itself at home. It feels a little more distant now.

"Thank you, Wren. I am... *so* glad I met you."

"Me too."

Chapter 8

LARK CANNOT REMEMBER THE last time that minutes and hours slipped away from them. But in this abandoned house, curled into Wren, there is a moment that stretches infinite where they truly believe that everything will be alright.

They almost mourn when Wren lets go and claims first watch. They do their best to hide it behind a half faked yawn.

The bed is pulled to the window so whoever is on watch can sit against the headboard and look out. Lark partially undresses to free themself from their binder, while Wren politely stares out of the window for the undignified removal period.

"I'll leave this off tomorrow," they say, after she turns back, "all that running today was... difficult."

Wren makes a sympathetic face. "Oh, yeah. Good call."

They climb back into the bed and lean against Wren's side. Sleep comes the moment their eyes close, faster than they can remember. The dreams that come are red hair and purple eyes

— a musical laugh echoes throughout and it is as agonising as expected, yet somehow more bearable.

It is a relief to be woken all the same. Lark and Wren switch places and Wren stretches her long body with a yawn so outrageous it is almost an operatic aria if the alto were stupendously drunk.

"Urgh," Wren says when Lark cannot restrain a giggle.

Once Wren is snoring into her pillow, and fondness is curling pleasantly in Lark's chest, they turn their attention to the view of the city. The lights from the temples shine so bright it can be seen anywhere within the walls, and other lanterns lit at random dot the cityscape.

In the pathetic way that has become so familiar, Lark's eyes deviate from the lights to take in the sky. The band of green stars twinkles, mysterious and taunting as ever, unseen by almost everyone at this time in the month. Lark can only wonder if Nightingale is watching them too, for the first time in three years.

Time moves at a snail's pace, seconds eventually becoming minutes and minutes taking an eternity to become hours. But at last, the sun begins to peek above the horizon and throw light across the sky. It snaps Lark out of the haze of counting.

Wren stirs within moments of the first ray of sunlight hitting her face. She regards Lark with a sleepy smile. "Good morning."

"Good morning, you funny little dawn riser."

"Years of practice. Farming town."

"Oh, yes. You'll have to take me one day."

Wren makes a noncommittal noise in her throat as she sits up. "It's not that interesting. You'd be bored in three hours. Not enough books."

Lark can only laugh at that, and they busy themselves getting Wren's armour back on. After that, Lark fishes their breastband out of their bag to replace the binder for the day. They mourn the comforting sensation of compression; breathing is a worthwhile trade, however.

"Do we have time for breakfast?" Wren asks. "It may be hard to catch her with an empty stomach."

"I'm sure we can find something on the way to the eastern city gates, to see if Palla's had any luck this morning."

Their heart pounds in their chest at the mere thought of coming face to face with Nightingale again. Wren being there, too, now understanding in a way that no one has before —

They had laid themself bare the night before. It's terrifying to dwell on, but Wren's smile has not yet changed, and so long as it does not, then perhaps all will be well.

Lark and Wren are halfway down the third street when they see the smoke. A pillar of grey kisses the sunrise and thickens with each few moments that pass.

"Is it her, do you think?" Wren asks, with urgency.

"We can't rule it out," Lark says. "Come on!"

The run towards danger, towards a problem that must be fixed, is always something that fills Lark with a primal joy they will not easily admit to. The surge in their chest is unparalleled, the frantic beat of their heart driving them forward every step, every leap.

Running towards where Nightingale might be? All the better, all the worse, all the more.

The column of smoke only continues to grow as Lark and Wren dash through the streets. Whatever is burning, it is no small tree. They keep running until they can see it; the target is a large but seemingly abandoned, irrelevant building on the northeast side of town. And every wall, column, and curtain, is ablaze.

"Oh," Wren says, staring at the inferno.

"Arson isn't Nightingale's style," Lark says, scanning the structure, "it isn't learning, it's destroying, this must be someone else, a strange coincidence, or a *distraction*—"

"Oh, Lark, are you *sure*?" calls a voice from on high.

Horror drops into Lark's stomach like a heavy stone. Nightingale is hanging from a spire on the roof, her figure drowned in smoke.

"I — what — what could you possibly learn from this?!" they ask.

Her laugh is all the more terrible for how it comes through the din, mixing with the crackle of the flames into a new form of Lark's nightmare.

"Whether or not you'll catch me," she says.

And she lets go of the spire. Gravity immediately snatches her from sight, yanking her into the heart of the blazing building.

"*Nightingale!*"

"Lark, no!"

Wren's shout is too late. Lark's body has already acted on instinct, jerking into action and driving them forward into the structure, everything else be damned.

The inside is far more decorated and furnished than Lark would have expected from the outside, but now it is all crumbling.

Lying on the floor is the still form of Nightingale. Against all reason and sense, Lark's heart wrenches in their chest. Control is an illusion; their feet are carrying them forward with no care for the smoke or heat.

"Nightingale," they say as they slide to the ground next to her. "Nightingale!" They touch her face with trembling fingertips.

Nightingale's eyes snap open. "Hello, darling," she says, with a smile brighter than it has any right to be. "How nice. You tried. You do care."

"Of course I care, it's never been about—" Lark stops as she sits up and puts their faces a mere two inches apart. Breathing gets more difficult than it already is. "You teleported. You were never in any — I'm so *stupid*."

"Well. Obviously. Although I would say gullible, over stupid." Nightingale's thumb traces over Lark's lips and their body shudders in response. "Should we get out of here, darling?"

A part of Lark *aches* for her, the part that never stopped, that has had to be pushed further and further down where no one can see as Nightingale saunters closer and closer to a point of no return. *One kiss,* it asks, *just one. It's been so long.* Nightingale's eyes are flicking between Lark's lips and their eyes and Lark begins to lean in, so that their foreheads touch. Something gives way in Lark's chest, a concession or confession or collapse —

The moment shatters when Lark coughs violently from the suffocating smoke. "The building is on fire!"

"I am, in fact, aware," Nightingale says wryly. "I did light it, after all."

"Why?" Lark staggers to their feet, their head spinning. They register a crash behind them but cannot tear their eyes from Nightingale. "Since when has arson been in your interest? Surely you didn't light this whole building on fire just to see if I would dive into it for you."

Nightingale smiles, but her body doubles over with a cough of her own. "It *is* a bit strange, isn't it? I wonder if you'll be able to figure it out."

The movement swings the mask hanging from her neck — her key to free movement among the guards of the city. *Take it, now, try,* a sensible part of their mind says. Lark reaches for the chain, to see if it could be broken easily.

Their hand closes over it, but Nightingale's hand curls on top.

"Tsk tsk, this isn't yours," she purrs, or tries to. It comes out as more of a wheeze. "You need to ask before touching a girl's special things."

Lark snorts. "You didn't use to mind."

"You didn't use to throw me in prison. We're both disappointed." Nightingale steps closer, grip on their hand tight, eyes locked with theirs. "But you can make it up to me, any time."

"I have heard *enough*, and seen too little," a new voice barks. "Now, Wren."

Chapter 9

WHAT FOLLOWS IS UNDIGNIFIED. Palla and Wren dash into the space and apprehend Nightingale and Lark respectively, dragging them from the building and putting their hands in cuffs behind their backs. Nightingale is shouting in any second she isn't coughing, fighting Palla all the way, but with her hands restrained she cannot cast her spells and her body alone might as well be a mouse's compared to Palla.

They all get out of the building. To Lark's surprise, Wren does not release her hold on them once they are in the open air.

"And to what do I owe this colourful treatment, Wren?" Lark asks, lightly.

"Uh," Wren's pale complexion is pink with embarrassment, "Palla says you both need to be taken into custody. She believes you're not taking the capture seriously. You might even be *helping* her, for all we know."

"For all *we* know?" Lark asks, eyebrow up. "I see. And since when do you work for the temple of War?"

"You know I don't," Wren retorts," and *I* know you're not helping her but... it didn't look great, Lark. I figure you can make a case to the Bishops. With me taking you, Palla could focus on her. And it worked, we got her. We got you both out of there before it collapsed on you."

To make her point, the rest of the roof chooses that moment to give in, like a resounding if overly dramatic exclamation point. Lark glances up to the sky and all around them, half expecting to hear the laughter of the Trickster god.

"Well, then," is all they manage to say, when they look back to a rare case of smug Wren.

"Or did you forget about that? Because you had your nice little chat going?"

Lark cannot admit to such a distinctly unimpressed Wren that yes, they had definitely entirely forgotten about that particular danger. They are determining what possible way they could sidetrack the conversation entirely when a pair of manacles is slapped on their wrist by Palla. The bar is passed to Wren for safekeeping.

"Just for a moment," Palla says, turning back to Nightingale whose manacle bar is in Palla's hand already.

A ring is on Nightingale's middle finger and Nightingale goes to the specific effort of raising it individually as Palla lifts the hand. Palla snorts and yanks the ring off. A small, dark gem glistens on the band.

"Found the magic blocker," Palla announces, turning the ring over in her fingers and tucking it into a pouch on her belt.

Nightingale sighs so loudly and dramatically that Lark cannot believe she is genuinely put out by the situation. For someone with smoke and soot covering most of her spectacles, she is as cool as a river.

"Can she teleport with those on?" Palla asks.

"If they're the same, regular manacles you have on me, yes," Lark says, "though the manacles would come with her. She needs to be able to see her destination. I would suggest a blindfold."

Nightingale whistles suggestively and Lark cannot help how their ears burn.

"You truly don't have anything to worry about," Nightingale says to them all as Palla ties cloth around her eyes. "I'm just happy to go for a nice walk. It's a good morning for it."

"And a nice morning for an interrogation to find out why *this place* was your target," Palla growls. She snatches the manacle bar from Wren so that she had them both in her personal control. "Now get moving."

"Is this place *important*?" Lark asks.

"No," Palla says immediately, but Nightingale giggles. "Alright, what do you know about—"

"Uh, Lark? Incoming," Wren interrupts.

A group of mages, all dressed in the blue and silver of the Winter Wolf, are rapidly approaching. Palla yanks them all back. The priests assemble in front of the burning building and begin a mass chant.

"You'll love this," Lark whispers to Wren.

Storm clouds gather, darker and thicker with every moment of chanting, and only right above them. Wren's eyes are wide and childlike. She watches with wonder as the clouds open and a torrent of rain is unleashed. The fire has no chance, no matter its ferocity. It is doused within a minute.

"Woah," Wren whispers. "Can you do that?"

"Gifted magic can only affect people, one way or another," Lark explains. "This lot aren't priests, they're Disciplined or Innate mages who work for the city."

"But they're in robes—"

"Yes, they're either naturally attuned to water and storm or have put in years of study to manipulate it, they're being polite and giving The Winter Wolf some due credit."

"It's the Theocracy, dear, it wouldn't be proper if the gods didn't get credit for everything, including things they haven't done at all," Nightingale drawls. "Wren, was it? You've been keeping my Lark company this last little while?"

"The last six months or so," Wren answers after a few moments of hesitation. "Met just before the war kicked off. Sticking together seemed even smarter once it did."

"How nice." Nightingale could be talking about the weather, or a piece of cake, or daydreaming about suffocating Wren to the point of death. It is impossible to tell. "I'd hate for them to be lonely, even if that's all *I've* known the last couple of years."

It is bait. It is needlessly, pointedly passive aggressive. Lark should know better than to rise to it, but they whip around with an entire ramble about *actions and consequences and you knew what you were doing when you did it, you know I wish things were different but it is impossible —*

And they are stuck. Nightingale's blindfold stops the words short, like a bucking horse, and the mental whiplash is intense enough that Lark's manacles rattle as they clutch their head and groan.

"Sorry, darling, what was that?" Nightingale asks. "Didn't catch it."

"Oh *shut up*," Wren tells her. "Some friend you are."

"At least I'm not a *pet*."

Palla yanks them along without any specific command, passing judgement with every glance, muttering to herself about academics with baggage and attitude problems and an allergy to common sense.

"You okay?" Wren asks Lark, hand on their shoulder.

Lark's head spins as they force their legs to keep pace with Palla. Their body is rebelling, wanting nothing more than to take off the blindfold and shake Nightingale until she admits who she pledged herself to, who began driving her to this madness and selfishness so beyond her own heights, who twisted the darkest parts of her into something so much more wretched.

A deep breath. A glance at Wren.

"I will be," Lark says. Because they need to be. Hope is essential, always, even if it is a painful companion at times.

The silence that follows is awful. The bright red and gold of Nightingale's smug satisfaction and sense of triumph is dancing in the entirety of Lark's field of vision. She's usually a dead spot, purposefully and expertly contained within and aware from their gaze.

So she wants them to see. Wants them to know how pleased she is.

With an odd ache in their chest, Lark realises that it is all she really has. If she cannot have Lark's attention, then what else is there?

"So you're the special one, then," Nightingale says to Palla, "the one all the big shots are talking about. The one with the big destiny."

Palla, although Lark would have thought it impossible, stiffens further. "How do you — the bishop."

Nightingale smiles. If her eyes were visible, Lark just knows that she would be fluttering her eyelashes.

"Fascinating place to be, a big fancy head like that," Nightingale says. "I got quite a bit of time to dig around in it. He might have a bit of a headache when they bring him back."

"This place is so weird. At home, resurrections are weird things in stories. But you killed him knowing they could bring him back right away," Wren says.

"Only because he's a bishop," Lark says, making a face. "Anyone else, in wartime, without a small fortune to donate? Good luck. You'd never think being cursed to be a goldfish would be fortunate, but... curse removal is easy by comparison."

"We don't have enough time or magic to resurrect all the warriors we need to as it is," Palla agrees.

"There's a time limit?" Wren asks. "Sorry. We didn't have any kind of real mage in our village at all. Just the usual little stuff."

"When you die, your spirit lingers in the vicinity, for a time," Lark says. "That's why a lot of funeral sites and customs last for days—"

"To keep the spirit company, I know," Wren says. "Right, so you can only bring them back while they're still lingering? About, what, within a week?"

"Usually. A few people have been known to do it after that time, but that's a whole other scale of magic."

"And they have to be willing to return."

"Yes." Lark shudders. "I'm sure some twisted people have found ways to engineer it outside of those rules, but I hate to think how that could go amiss."

"I'm sure your *friend* could think of something." Palla's voice is scathing.

"Please," Nightingale scoffs, "I kill people so that they tell me things and stay dead. I have better things to do than to drag people back into the world kicking and screaming. How dull. The living are whiny enough as it is."

"Gods, this walk has never felt so long," Palla mutters to herself. Lark is inclined to agree.

They are in the centre of the city now, still far too long to go for Lark's comfort. As a group they seem to have exhausted things to say to each other, a simmering of frustration bubbling under everyone's skin for various reasons. So... pointed silence it is.

Pointed silence soon broken by a deafening roar overhead.

Chapter 10

IT IS AN EERIE, chilling thing to hear a city scream in unison. The cacophony is instant and swells in time with the beat of the wings and a second roar. Lark's heart stops for a moment. Above them, a shape of glittering green soars and spirals. It's larger even than the dragon who had been the original owner of Lark's eye.

Do they see the fear down here? Smell it?

The sickly, pale yellow is creeping in from every corner, like a gas infecting the city, tinging Lark's vision and making them dizzy.

Guards are running and shouting. Palla's hands have gone for her shield and axe. The dragon passes the city and Lark waits for it to circle back. They know they should run or take cover or do *something* but that is an illusion of agency in the face of a creature like this. Without even knowing what kind of breath it has, preparation is near impossible. Ice? Fire? Lightning? Acid? Poison?

"Wait, *shit*!" Palla whirls around and her eyes widen as she scours the group. The group that now consists of three people and a blindfold on the cobblestones.

"Sorry, got to dash," Nightingale's voice says with a laugh. "Why don't you go and deal with that pesky dragon?"

They all whirl around to see Nightingale on a nearby rooftop, hands still in the barred manacles but now free of Palla and Lark. She is grinning, fierce and joyful. A jump, high in the air, with a portal beneath her. She falls through it only to appear higher in the air, a few feet ahead, pulling her manacled hands under her legs mid jump so they can rest in front of her… and Nightingale finishes it off by blowing Lark a kiss.

"See you later, darling, I'm sure."

Bells begin to ring out across the city, declaring the emergency of the dragon's appearance. They serve as a strange accompaniment for Nightingale's escape, a herald of disaster she can bring as well as any mighty scaled beast.

When Nightingale teleports to the next roof and begins running, Lark is caught staring after her and is not prepared for how they are slammed into the wall of the nearest building.

"Ow," Lark complains, blinking until their vision shows a fuming Palla. "Ah. Palla. Hello."

"She is my charge, not the dragon, and she is getting away," Palla says. Her voice is low and dangerous. "If I release you, so you can assist in the chase with that tracking spell of yours, this is your last chance. Prove to me that you're on our side, not hers."

"Then let's stop wasting time."

Palla hesitates, and unlocks the manacles. Lark takes only a moment to rub their wrists before grabbing their amulet and reaching out to the Scholar, focusing on how Nightingale is what they must seek.

The spell takes hold and shifts the axis of Lark's world with its pull.

"This way!"

The three of them break into a sprint. Anyone they pass on the streets is shaken by the dragon and questions are thrown at Palla in a neverending bombardment.

"Ser! The dragon! What should we do?!"

"Follow the procedure and *get inside*!" Palla barks to them. "It's taking its time coming back around, so use that time! Go!"

Over and over, to dozens of panicked people as they weave through street after street, she repeats this. Some beseech her, thank her, all by name. The whole while, Palla doesn't slow.

Nightingale is still in view but only just. The roofs ahead of them are serving as a clear runway.

"Should I follow her on the roofs?" Wren asks Lark.

"She'd probably just teleport back down to make it a waste of your time," Lark says.

As they run, Palla is rummaging with her belt and pockets, her shield tucked under one arm to manage the awkwardness as she runs. It is an impressive, baffling endeavour that Lark suspects any inquiry into will result in their head getting bitten off.

It is after another few minutes of the chase that they are coming up to a bridge, and Nightingale vanishes from the rooftop on the other side. Palla glances back behind her, eyes flashing.

"Lark, where is she?"

Lark touches the amulet again and checks the magic, tunes into it further. "Still here, somewhere close. She's stopped."

Palla stalks across the bridge ahead of them. Her axe and shield drawn, each heavy step echoing as she advances like a bear about to strike. "Come on out," she calls, "the running must be getting boring. Wouldn't fighting me be more fun? Don't I have something you want back? Being tracked is going to be tiring soon."

"Palla, please don't underestimate her magic," Lark shouts. "You know she's *deadly*—"

"So am I," Palla retorts, voice and face wearing dark confidence and a touch of malice. "So, may the best woman win."

Her own symbol, the claw across a shield of War, centers the prayer Palla utters next. A glow covers Palla's axe and the surface of her armour.

Lark's rampant curiosity is itching to see it in action; every other part of them is screaming out that it will fall short into nothing, that Nightingale will not engage. Perhaps Palla is right about her own skill, but Lark does not want her dead any more or less than Nightingale.

Palla is halfway through her step off the bridge when Nightingale appears behind her.

"Alright then, I will," Nightingale says, making a swipe for the pouch where Palla had stored the magic blocking ring.

She has to jump back when Palla swings around with surprising speed. The magic of the blessing shimmers across Palla's eyes.

Lark has seen battles between mages and great warriors before. They are strange things, often more won by circumstance as they are seldom the right match or display of skill — the warrior is useless if they cannot get close, while any mage will struggle to complete the intricate physical actions needed to channel and release magic if they are constantly dodging strikes an inch from their head. Sometimes it is just a matter of speed, of who can keep the ball in their court, keep the fight on their terms.

This battle is none of those things. Battle may even be the wrong word. Palla is roaring and swinging the axe in strong, deadly strokes that could slice Nightingale in half if they catch her out. Nightingale, however, wields no offensive magic. Nothing at all.

Duck. Duck. Sidestep. Open a portal and slip through a moment before her head is separated from her shoulders. Repeat.

Nightingale is laughing. Nightingale is dancing.

In this awful, shining moment a part of Lark is jealous of Palla — fiercely, desperately, idiotically. But Lark and Wren are frozen on the sidelines, able only to watch for fear of meeting the axe's wrath by accident.

Nightingale ducks the axe again. The next swing collides with her arm and not a word leaves her mouth but her body goes off kilter. Palla swings and Nightingale's feet push against the cobblestones to launch herself backward. The axe scrapes across her stomach, or where her stomach had been a half second before; Lark cannot see from their angle.

Nightingale drops and rolls into a portal that takes her back several paces. There, on one knee, wisps of shadow finally form around her hand, bubbling into the thickness that Lark knows can suffocate. Palla, seeing this, gears up a charge.

One dash. One swing. One circle around.

The pouch from Palla's belt comes away with Nightingale's hand as the mage ducks and misses the axe by a hair.

"Predictable swing," Nightingale laughs. A new portal takes her to a nearby roof. "Thanks ever so much for—"

A pebble lands in her hand as she empties the pouch. The laughter dies.

Palla smirks. "Predictable swing."

The ever present, indomitable grin of Nightingale's turns into a small, dangerous smirk. "Well played," she says, like there is glass in her throat.

She teleports back in front of Palla and the dance begins anew. It is dizzying to watch — the blur of the axe, the flashes of amethyst magic. It is an odd crescendo of a thing, building to something that even Lark cannot see.

Palla is pure fury, lit up with red in various shades. Nightingale is focus, so much focus that Lark can only examine the hues and try to see what she is planning, what is worth almost losing her head.

There is a strong downward swing from Palla, aimed for Nightingale's outstretched arms. Nightingale, whose stillness had been suspicious, twists herself in the last moment.

The axe comes down on the manacle bar and splits it in two. Nightingale grins, fierce and beautiful.

"Thanks ever so much, dear," she says to Palla, who growls and tries another swing, but Nightingale is gone in a moment. From the roof, she blows a kiss to Lark and makes a quick exit.

Palla shouts, wordless and horrified, and drops to one knee. Lark and Wren dash to her side as she pants from the exertion of it all.

"Are you alright?" Lark asks. "Good job on moving the blocker."

"So long as she doesn't have it, you can find her," Palla says. "So *find her*. Don't make me regret taking your binds off."

"She's going to come back for it," Lark tells her. "She knows she'll never have a moment's peace from me without it. But she'll likely want to get the rest of the manacles off first."

What follows is Lark's least favourite type of silence — the one where ideas are needed and none come, where glances of uncertainty are exchanged instead of words.

Finally, however, Wren speaks. "Why don't we set up an ambush? If she's going to come back for Palla and the blocker... we could put Palla at one of the city exits. Then it's on her way out too. How could she resist?"

Palla's eyes light up. Her smile is unnerving. "And I can have some of my people stationed to help bring her down."

"If you and your people could try to use non-lethal force, however," Lark says, and a glint of red stops their words dead as they glance at Palla's axe. A sheen of blood covers its edge. *Oh.*

Palla follows their gaze and scowls. "She doesn't afford us the same luxury."

"No, but you're not a criminal we're trying to arrest, one would hope there is a point of difference somewhere," Lark retorts.

"... we'll see how it goes," Palla says, and it is clear that there will not be more to it than that. "Very well. I'll get it arranged. I'll be there, ready, in an hour. If you think you can stall her. Direct her. Whatever it takes to get her there at the right time."

Lark coughs. "I'm... sure I can think of something."

Palla's aura shifts between determination and annoyance as she rolls her eyes. "I'm sure. Get moving. It doesn't look like that dragon is coming back, gods be thanked, but I want to check in on the situation all the same."

With that, she departs. Lark restarts the location spell and begins directing Wren north.

"How would she be getting the manacles off? Threaten a blacksmith?" Wren asks.

"Perhaps," Lark says with a snort that dies too early. "I — I don't know. I don't know. I—"

Wren stops and puts herself in their path. "Are you okay?" Lark opens their mouth to lie and is fixed with such a firm look that their lips press shut again. "This is not the time to keep it to yourself."

"As opposed to what, Wren?" Lark asks, frustration bubbling in their chest. The lack of discomfort from the binder, usually a helpful sensation for centering themself and keeping everything in check, leaves them feeling vulnerable. "Am I okay? What a diminutive question for such a situation. I'm not, not really. How could I be?"

"You can talk to me."

"I did. Last night I told you things I have never told *anyone,* Wren. Please appreciate that. But I will not unravel my heart for you to examine when there is no cure for this ailment."

"We have a plan now," Wren reminds them earnestly. "We'll get her."

"Yes, no, I'm feeling wonderful about sending her into an ambush full of devoted followers of War who like to hit first and do the paperwork later." Lark begins to pace back and forth in front of where Wren has planted herself. "I know she doesn't deserve the mercy, I know she would never spare any of them a second glance, but mercy is not *deserved.* That is the whole point. We have to be better than her, or we are lost to it all."

"I'm... sure she'll be fine."

"Oh, quite probably," Lark says, mouth fully ignited and unable to be stopped while their arms swing wildly in gesture, "but how many of them would she have to kill to be so? That isn't better! And that is assuming I even manage to think of some incredibly clever way to trick her into going there in the first place. Assuming she won't see through anything I try, assuming she won't kill you the moment she sees you—"

Wren's hands come down on Lark's shoulders and hold them still. "Lark. Breathe."

It should be easier without the binder; Lark is used to the shallower breaths that come with wearing it. But in this moment, though the breaths are full, it's like they are empty. Empty of everything that Lark needs from them. No oxygen. No calm. No clarity.

"There's no scenario where I win," Lark says, in a tired whisper. "The best case is that I put the only person who has ever truly understood me back in a cage underground."

Wren pulls them into a tight hug. Lark sighs into it and clutches the top ridge of her armour, their fingertips curling around the warm metal.

"I'm sorry," Wren murmurs. Her deep voice calms something in Lark's chest. "I wish I had any better ideas."

"You've already had the best one. Using Palla to lure her out? It's fantastic. You're fantastic. It's simply an impossible situation."

Wren gradually releases the hug and holds Lark's gaze. "It might not be the same... but other people can know you. We can do our best to understand you, if you let us try. Maybe it would always be second. But it would be better than nothing, better than this. Not a replacement but... something new."

It should be a revelation. It should be sacrilege. The idea of not needing Nightingale somehow, the idea that someone else like Wren could fill that void or something close... instead of imploding anything, it simply bounces off and falls, an idea to be picked up and tucked away in a pocket for later, for when Lark has the time to turn it over in their hands and make sense of it.

Lark swallows. "I — yes. Thank you, Wren. For... everything."

"Of course. Now. What's the plan? Do you really think she'll kill me if I get close?"

"I think that it is dangerous to assume anything, with her. And I won't gamble with your safety."

"But you'll gamble with your own?"

The question actually pulls a chuckle from Lark's throat. "Oh, always. But she won't hurt me. Not seriously. She would find a world without me in it entirely too dull, I expect."

Wren purses her lips. "So you want to go and see her alone. That's where you're going with this. Are you sure that's a good idea?"

"I just — I just have to try, Wren." Lark licks their lips. "It's so hard to say. I might be able to convince her to stop. To wait. She wants me to come with her, and I never would, but she is still my friend. She might come with me. I don't know. I don't know."

The frown creasing Wren's forehead and tensing her mouth is telling enough, but her aura is pale yellow with disbelief and concern. To her credit, all she says is, "Alright. Good luck, then. Don't you *dare* get hurt."

Lark smiles. Gratitude flutters in their chest and stutters only when Wren's fingers push the front of Lark's hair behind their ear. Her hands, as always, are startlingly warm.

"Where do you need me to be?" she asks, voice soft.

"Take one of the other entrances, close to Palla's one. Just in case it doesn't work. But do not, under any circumstances, engage Nightingale if she comes."

Wren nods. She steps back, turns, and walks away.

Lark is left alone with their treachery and a final, fleeting hope.

Chapter 11

SOLITUDE HAS BECOME A rare sensation. The odd freedom, the lack of accountability, the not having to hide how they immediately turn their head towards the magical trace on Nightingale. A sigh fills their chest with longing and empties it a moment later, too dangerous to hold onto for more than one moment.

"I'm on my way," Lark says, as if Nightingale might be able to hear.

They run. Memories follow them, catching up as they sprint alongside, Nightingale's laughter in Lark's ears. It is so easy, *too* easy, to remember. Nightingale, all but twenty, her hair bouncing with each stride and purple eyes alight. Words tumbling out of her mouth. Some excitable anecdote about a professor not realising their mistake and continuing to teach the entire class wrong.

The past follows Lark through each alley, each turn, echoing around every corner.

"We'll be okay, won't we?" comes a memory. Nightingale's voice had been tentative in a way it had so seldom been then. Her parents had already begun to ignore her, then, in favour of her older sister who had stayed serving the Life Giver, who was *such a promising acolyte.* Her conversion to follow the Scholar had just been another division to add to the pile.

"Of course. We're Lark and Nightingale. We're going to be amazing," Lark had said.

Was I always a stepping stone to you? They wonder now.

The location spell is still going strong. It's also been constant — Nightingale has stopped somewhere. Lark keeps their fingers crossed and tries to weave some kind of protection around their heart, anything to keep them focused. It is not as simple as the university infatuation, the graduate devotion, that it had once been.

The first body. The first secret, hidden well but never forever. The many, many more that have followed. Blood stains stark on Nightingale's skin, the scent of iron lingering well into the night, refusing to leave Lark's nostrils and forcing their dinner out of their body. Then came the bodies that shed no blood at all, suffocated by her growing power, the darkness like oil.

The eyes behind her glasses that, simply, did not see any of it as a problem. With everything they are, Lark misses everything those eyes used to be. They mourn that they will never see her shrouded in the dark grey of regret. That it is an impossible sight and thus the thing Lark will wish for until they are without breath.

"Idiot," they mutter to themself.

Their search and spell has brought them to a door. It is simple, the front of a house, the doormat hosting letters unopened. Different date stamps. Owners clearly out of town.

Deep breath. Lark does their best to collect everything they are and stand for, and steps inside.

Their quarry sits on a couch, a bottle and small basket in front of her. Her shirt is pulled up to reveal her stomach, which bears an angry red line. The knot that has been in Lark's stomach ever since seeing the blood on Palla's axes loosens. The injury could be much worse.

"Hello, darling," Nightingale says as the door closes.

Lark stares. "She got you."

"Not badly," Nightingale says, shrugging. "Or my guts would have led you the whole way here. But enough to sting. Still, if you'll dance with an axe..."

Lark moves to sit next to her. It feels as though they've swallowed a live canary who is taking up a tap dancing career.

"Hello," is all they say, as Nightingale glances up from where she is dabbing the wound with alcohol. Her casual curiosity fades into a second of tenderness.

"Hello."

"May I?" Lark asks.

The cloth is passed over and Lark wrings it out. Nightingale's gaze is heavy. Lark presses the cloth to the wound and resists every urge to glance up, temptation and fear mingling in a hurricane in their chest.

"You look well," Nightingale says.

This presents a problem. Lark cannot reply without —

Their traitorous eyes flick up, because they have to. "Thank you. You are looking..." The pause to consider the answer, to gather the information necessary for it, forces their words to screech to a halt. Nightingale is gaunt, shadows under her eyes and body now too thin to be healthy. But her eyes are bright as ever, her hair still rich and colourful if greasy. "Good. Better than expected. Considering."

She snorts, and the smile that curls her mouth is so distracting that Lark forces themself to concentrate on their work and hands once again. No more talking. No more looking. Just working. Helping. Healing. Healing a murderer. Only by mundane means, as Lark does not have the backbone to ask the Scholar to lend their magic to heal someone as corrupted as Nightingale. But even so.

"Good considering you put me in prison for three years?" Nightingale asks, pleasantly. Lark runs their tongue over their teeth to fight the urge to reply, and the nausea that comes with attempting to speak without eye contact. "If it helps at all, darling, no hard feelings."

Lark does not reply but they look up just long enough to give her a sceptical eyebrow raise. Or at least, that is the plan. Her hand cups their face as it tilts, her thumb brushing over the scales around the dragon eye. Lark's entire body shudders, stutters, and forgets every plan. They stay frozen, a prisoner to her gaze.

"Life is complex. You and I have known this a long while now. We all have obligations. To ourselves, to our values, to our urges. How can I fault you for yours, when I cannot deny my own?"

"I—"

"Of course, faulting me for mine seems to be the song you're singing. But I suppose I'm just the bigger person."

That breaks the spell Lark is caught in — the spell of their own sentimentality. The sparks of annoyance and indignance catch and Lark rolls their eyes.

"Whatever helps you sleep at night, dear," they say.

"Oh, I've never had any trouble sleeping, since our little ascension," Nightingale says brightly. "I get the most interesting dreams. Visions of things so beyond imagination they can only be real. Gifts. Foresight. Something."

"From your little benefactor?"

"Perhaps."

Bitterness is an awful emotion. So negative, so likely to lead to unnecessary unpleasantness. But at this point it is impossible to be impartial and polite. It is not a new argument; it has been waiting on a shelf for years and festering. It has grown infestations of desire and loneliness and regret.

Lark catches her wrist in their hand. "Is there anything I could have done? *Anything*? Is there a way we might not have ended up here, that you might not have chosen them, whoever or whatever they are?"

Nightingale has a mighty control over herself — at least, in a few specific ways. Anyone can theoretically try to hide their emotional aura from Lark's view, to keep it tight within themselves, and some manage it without even knowing they're doing it. (Of course, most have no idea that there is an aura reader around, and don't think to try.) Ever since Nightingale had helped Lark with the messy process of swapping one of their eyes for the dragon one, she had shown an aptitude for tucking her emotions away within herself where Lark could not see.

In this moment she is more colourful than Lark has seen her in years. There are tiny flares of different shades of red — conflict and a touch of frustration. Her hand comes up again, her fingertips brushing over the skin of Lark's cheek, over the golden scales that are so sensitive. Then she takes a hold that is tight, too tight, and Lark cannot help the gasp that leaves them.

"Unless you have discovered the key to turning back the wheel of time itself," Nightingale says, voice low and strange before her face twists into a scowl, "that is an astoundingly stupid question."

"I — no, it isn't."

"Are you torturing yourself over this? Wondering if *there is something you could have done?* It's done. It cannot be changed. We both made our choices. I agreed to what I agreed to, and we launched ourselves into the unknown, and that is the course of events."

Emotion chokes Lark's throat. "I was just... wondering."

"You're one of the most brilliant minds this city has ever produced. Wonder about something else." Nightingale's eyes flash. In bitter resentment she is awful and wonderful and Lark cannot breathe. "You have a *Wayfinder*. I know that's what they gave you for catching me. Think of what you could be doing and instead you're running around with some silly girl with a sword—"

"Wren is my friend."

"And yet, here you are, talking to me."

"You're my friend too."

"Am I?" Nightingale's grip on Lark's cheek loosens and she runs a hand over their hair, all at once the most gentle touch Lark can ever remember receiving. "Why did you come here, Lark? Why did you come to see me?"

There are words. Lark knows words, knows them intimately, how to decipher them and weave them together. They all seem out of reach now, as Nightingale leans in, her breath hot against their skin, her fingers sliding down the back of their neck. The shiver that goes down Lark's spine is violent and humiliating. Blood rushes up their neck and around their ears.

"Oh, my love," Nightingale murmurs, "whatever are we to do with each other?"

"I don't know," Lark says, with a single soft breath.

"Run in circles for years to come?" Her other hand slides up Lark's knee and along their thigh, firm through the soft fabric. She leans closer to whisper in their ear. "Take each other when they're not looking? I won't tell if you don't."

Lark's brain ceases to function for a full three seconds as blood courses all through them at breakneck speed. It pounds in their temples like drums of warning. *Danger. Danger. Danger.*

It has been so long since they have done anything like *that*. For so long Lark had thought that they simply had no inclination at all, then as they had grown closer to Nightingale they had finally begun to feel what so many others had talked about. That pull, that desire, the way the walls of the room seem to close in when they're close. But, so far, it has only ever, ever been her.

Lark's hand closes over Nightingale's, stopping it in its tracks. "I can't."

Nightingale smiles. The flare of blue melancholy is bright and brief. "I know. You have your part to play, and I have mine. Probably best we don't go off script."

Her nails dig into the back of Lark's neck to the point of pain. Then come the words, those terrible grating words of unknown origin, said with such fervour and conviction. Her eyes flash with purple as her hand in theirs slips free easily and summons shadows.

And then Lark can't breathe. It has come to this only once before, the first time it had all come to blows and tears and shouting and leaving. The darkness tastes tainted against Lark's mouth and prevents all smell.

Nightingale is not smiling anymore. Her face is awful, unyielding ice.

"It's been nice," she says, the sweetness in her voice misaligned with those terrible eyes and the darkness clawing at Lark's vision. "But I've done my time in a cage. I want to fly. If you'd ground me, then we are not the friends we wish to be."

Please, they want to say. But they have no idea what it is they are asking for anymore.

A new pain. Sharpness in their belly, her quill, buried but for a moment. The darkness closes in and Lark is lost.

Chapter 12

THE SANCTUM OF THE library. Bookshelves cradle them in privacy and nothing but knowledge itself. More of a home than any house either of them have known, their secret place, corners of whispers and hushed laughter. Lark's back hits the hard wood of a shelf, as Nightingale pushes them into it and relishes how they squeak. Her lips are warm and eager and she laughs at how they squirm before their hands lose themselves in her hair. A first year sees them and makes a comical noise before hurrying off and they pay no mind at all.

Thesis defense. A panel, an audience, and the pressure of their future laid out before them but for the hurdle of this challenge. But Lark has never given doubt a leg to stand on before, and this is something else altogether. They were made to do this, to prove their cleverness. They learn and believe and absorb as pure religion and letting the words flow out like this feels like flying. They are almost dazed when it is over and they come back down. In the front row Nightingale's eyes blaze with pride. Nightingale's turn after. If

Lark is flight then she is fire, passion infusing every word. Lark now always remembers what they had tried to forget — the first seed of doubt. Her topic choice, fascinating but disturbing. Her argument, excellent but extreme. Her eyes, dark and frenzied.

Lark's magic, a gift from the Scholar to be treasured, blossoms and grows. It begins to reach new heights, rivalling lower bishops. The praise is nice, to be sure, but they are still happiest alone and buried in a book. Nightingale, meanwhile, has her magic from the Scholar come in late, and not as powerful. (Or so she had said.) But she is blessed with a light that reveals the truth of things, revealing illusions and hidden meaning and so many other things. It is a truly wonderful gift, but Lark's magic can do so much more. Perhaps they should have been suspicious at how little she minded the imbalance between them. But she was so quick to push Lark that bit further, always fostering their talent further. Besides, magic is just one aspect of the world; they had so much to research.

Tenderness. Lark has never dreamed of such tenderness, of touch like this, of the bliss it can bring. Soft fingertips across their skin, Nightingale's lips following them, always so gentle, always treating them like a treasured discovery. Sanctuary. Being alone with her, and so understood, so supported, is sanctuary.

Graduation, excursion, exploring now as Seekers. The world all theirs for the taking. The dragon corpse is the find of a lifetime. The recovery of the eye starts as a challenge, a test of their regenerative and healing magic. The flesh stitches itself back together in Lark's hands, sealing itself at every tear with a soft glow, regaining the spark of magic within as it becomes whole. And then another challenge: to seize a dragon eye's power, a green dragon's insight, or to not? It had been a gory, painful process. Absolute trust required: lying back on a rock while Nightingale looms over them with a knife, the dragon eye in Lark's hand ready to replace their own. And after the mess, and the healing, and wrestling the magic of the eye into submission... a whole new view of the world. Seeing Nightingale glowing with gold and purple, washed in wonder even as blood covers both of their hands. That night had been... passionate.

The day that changed everything. "What is it you think is in here, anyway?" they ask her as they enter the strange ruin, months later. She simply shrugs, and they suspect she has an idea, but could never guess the extent of the deception. Could never know how far away she already is in so many ways even while her hand rests in theirs.

A light. A crack of searing light in darkness, in their mind, in the world — in something that is somehow both and neither. Their hand burning with the raw magic it touches. Waking up on a stone floor, head spinning, mouth fumbling to ask Nightingale if she is okay, if she saw and felt it all, and the words not leaving their mouth. The first instance of speech stuck in their throat.

The world is different now. The green stars shine every night above them and it is glorious, but every full moon brings a second moon to the sky. No one else can see it. They have, well and truly, risen to unthinkable heights. History is at their fingertips in new ways... but objects are so much easier to find than corpses. Lark's words are stubborn and particular and Nightingale has to invest in notebook after notebook and her shorthand ascends to new levels.

But the higher you fly, the further you fall. The lies pile up. Truths begin to emerge, and bodies unaccounted for. The beginning of the end.

An argument of tears and shouting and pleading on both sides. It ends on a slammed door and furious indecision. Within a week, Lark begins to chase her over the top half of the known world, through Qelandia, the Federation, and into Aesheim. Their only advantage is that she never expected them to come after her, to have the guts.

The cell door closes and Lark's last look at her yields purple eyes shining with tears of heartbreak and fury. They make sure she is taken care of.

"I've done my time in a cage. I want to fly. If you'd ground me, then we are not the friends we wish to be."

Lark wakes.

Their lungs burn and their head feels like a spinning top. Tears spring up immediately, stinging their eyes, and now that they have started they cannot stop. Years of agony, of longing, of wishing and trying and hoping, now spill into the world in the only form they can. When the emotion overflows the tears themselves it shifts into a scream instead, a strangled anguish in their throat.

I want to fly. If you'd ground me —

Lark curses her name. Her mysterious patron. Every word she has ever spoken. Their vision is tinted black and blue — their own emotions so powerful the waves of it are flowing in and out like tidal waves.

The world is dizzying. They catch their breath between words, words that fly free with no intended audience, a small mercy. Lark's hand touches their shirt. Wet. Sticky. Red.

It's an absurd thing, to belatedly recall one's own stabbing. Perhaps more so, to be lamenting the stain and tear of the clothing more than the wound. But it is only a delay, another few minutes Nightingale has brought herself, nothing more.

Lark's hand finds the coffee table and uses it to clamber to their feet. Then it is one hand on their holy symbol and one hand on their bleeding side.

"Scholar," they murmur, reaching for that magic and connection over unfathomable distance, "hear me, please. Stitch this flesh, seal this wound, return the strength I will so desperately need."

The warmth shifts and flares and the relief from the pain makes Lark gasp.

"Thank you, thank you," they say, mind racing faster than the body can follow. They are not fully healed but there is no time to wait for it to all come perfectly together.

There is, perhaps, no time at all. Lark runs from the house. Their head pounds in a syncopated harmony to their heart. Together they sound an awful song, a truth.

You might not ever get her back, their head sings, *she might be too far gone.*

Until now Lark had never actually accepted it as a possibility. It hurts more than Nightingale's stiletto quill ever could.

Not fair, Lark's heart beats, *not fair, not fair.*

A new section, a new melody, sweeping and tragic and threatening to pull Lark under forever. The beat, instead, is *life is not fair. Time to be strong. Life is not fair. Time to be strong.*

Chapter 13

IT IS A SPECIAL kind of cruelty, to come terms with perhaps needing to let Nightingale go while still having to chase her, while feeling the very magical core of themselves pulled towards her in the most guttural way.

Holding the Scholar's amulet at least provides a modicum of comfort. And there is another thing, something that brings a small tug of pride to Lark's chest. The direction of the spell. Nightingale is headed straight for the gate where Palla is stationed. Wren had been right.

Lark weaves through the streets and is so focused on the spell that every corner fades from their mind the moment it is passed. Non-essential information discarded to keep everything pertinent when their brain is so fuzzy otherwise.

A figure walks into their path.

"Oh, thank the gods, there you — oh, fuck," Wren says. "What happened to *she won't hurt me, Wren?*"

"I said she wouldn't *kill* me, if we're going to get pedantic about it," Lark retorts. They keep walking and Wren falls into quick, urgent step with them. "Your plan is working, Wren. She's headed for the gate. For Palla. She—"

"Did talking to her help?"

Lark shuts up, flushing with mortification, the grey and orange of their shame bright in their own vision but thankfully outside of Wren's perception. "It was..." How to even describe it? Honesty? Did they even know how to be totally honest with themself about it yet? "... enlightening. But there's nothing for it. We have to stop her, no matter what it takes."

"Good. We can do it. I'm with you."

Lark hears the words. But in the same moment they see the gate and come to a halt. Bodies litter the cobblestones toward the city exit, dark armour of the temple of War prevalent. With the full body armour and the distance it is impossible to say if they are all dead or simply unconscious. Not knowing is worse.

"Gods," Wren mutters under her breath.

"Still with me?" Lark asks. Their voice comes out too high, too hysterical, too close to a laugh in order to avoid a total breakdown.

Wren's hand clasps their shoulder with a firm and comforting squeeze. "Always. I'm here."

"Try-hard *bitch*!" someone ahead of them shouts.

Lark has never heard Nightingale sound quite so *put out* before. It is uncertain what it says about their current point of sanity that this is the first thing that crosses their mind as they launch themselves forward.

History is repeating; Nightingale and Palla are engaged in another deadly, lightning-fast duel. Neither have lost much ground or blood, it seems — only their composure.

"You're not walking out of here breathing," Palla seethes.

"Funny, that's what I said to your little friends there," Nightingale says, with a giggle that morphs into a shriek as Palla's axe narrowly misses her nose. "But you know. Trying to tell jokes to followers of War. Bit of an uphill battle. More so than actually *battling* them, anyway."

For all the laughter, she now truly looks the part of the deranged, escaped criminal she is so determined to play. Hands stained with crimson, hair wild and tangled all around her, jacket torn in too many places to count. Her glasses are crooked and playing a dangerous game with gravity.

Teleport. Teleport. Swing. Once again, getting closer is a sure way to lose a limb or get the wrong person killed. Lark and Wren are stuck, waiting for a change, an opening.

Teleport, near-miss, *stab*.

Nightingale's tiny stiletto finds a gap in the plates of armour and Palla yells. She swings wildly but Nightingale has embraced her from behind in a twisted power play — one that keeps her in a place of temporary safety.

"These dances are so special to me," Nightingale purrs. "I might even remember your name for more than a week." There is a shift in her arm and another gasp from Palla.

Her other hand explores, roaming the pouches on Palla's person with the urgency and efficiency of a pirate looting a sinking ship. Out comes the tiny ring and Nightingale kisses the shining metal before slipping it onto her finger.

In her single-minded greed, however, she has forgotten an essential detail. Palla's physical strength is so beyond her own that all the warrior needs is the right opening.

A sweep of the leg. A thrust of Palla's body weight backward. Nightingale hits the ground. Palla lands on top of her and the weight of the muscle and the armour has Nightingale gasping for air. Arms trapped. No portal this time.

"Good job, Palla," Lark says, reaching for their amulet, mentally mapping the hand motions for a spell that can help hold Nightingale in place, quiet her body and mind long enough to get her back to prison. "Hold her still, and in a minute I'll have her." They begin to utter the incantation, their fingers weaving the magic in the air.

Meanwhile, the conflict is shifting. The two women are locked in a primal struggle on the ground, both trying to get a better hold of the other. Nightingale's quill shines with blood but only finds metal plates it cannot penetrate in its new position. Palla has rolled over so her gauntleted hands can close around Nightingale's neck.

"Oh!" Nightingale chokes. "Hello."

Lark wants to tell Palla that it isn't necessary, that the spell will be done soon, but they cannot without having to restart. Still, Nightingale is doing a decent if undignified job of grabbing at Palla's hands with her own, holding them at bay as much as she can, preventing her neck being snapped on the spot.

Ten more seconds. Nine. Eight. Seven. The magic reaches for Nightingale's mind, ready to cradle it into induced tranquility so her body can follow it. Three. Two. One —

Lark clutches their head as the magic rebounds against their mind like a whip.

"Nice try, darling," Nightingale says, voice raspy. "My mind is better protected than ever."

A whine of pain escapes her, a half cough. One of her hands leaves Palla's for a moment to grab Palla by the chin and nose. With her last bit of spare breath she exhales an incantation.

The thick, insidious darkness bubbles from her fingertips and covers the bottom half of Palla's face. The roar that follows is muffled and furious. Palla's hands try to press tighter — nausea dances in Lark's stomach at the realisation that Palla is, without a doubt, trying to kill Nightingale with her bare hands. The struggle gets slower, and tighter, until neither move but for small jerks of the head and the pull of Nightingale's hands against Palla's gauntlets, the desperate tugs that are weak but *just* enough to buy more time for her neck.

Lark has seen many incomprehensible, horrifying things. It is hard to recall them now, when faced with a mutual destruction like this. Each moment that passes they expect a change. A falter. Anything. But it doesn't come.

Both women without air, both refusing to waver. A tiny pained cry from Nightingale as something snaps. Her hand, changing angle and continuing to pull regardless.

"Oh for — neither of you are going to walk away, if you keep this up," Wren says.

Lark scrambles for a solution. Whatever could turn this situation into something better. Something salvageable.

One is a headstrong hero. The other, a remorseless killer. Both unique, both unbelievably skilled. Anything, anything at all, is better than losing them both.

"Wren, on my count," Lark whispers as they summon the Scholar's light into their hand, "separate them." Wren nods. "One. Two. Three."

Lark hurls the magic at Palla and Nightingale. They both yell with the last of their strength, the holy magic burning them just enough for a moment of weakness in their grip. Wren pulls Palla off Nightingale and throws her onto the nearby ground.

Nightingale sputters and stumbles, gasping. Colourful bruises are already forming on the delicate skin of her neck. The darkness begins to slide from Palla's face but a scowl and a twist of Nightingale's hand later, and its position resets.

Palla writhes.

"Nope," Wren says, grabbing Nightingale and putting her hands behind her back. "Let her go. Nobody else needs to die."

"I disagree, she's extremely annoying," Nightingale retorts, in a wheeze instead of her usual voice.

Lark comes forward and kneels in front of her so that they are less than a foot apart. "Nightingale, please, it's over. Let this go."

"Over?" Nightingale cackles, and the spark in her eyes is familiar. It had been common back in university. Smugness, superiority, when she has found something before they have. "Oh, Lark, darling. It's just *beginning*."

"You're about to go back to prison. I won't let you hurt anyone else."

"That isn't what I meant, dearest, but first of all... no. I'm not. Unless you're about to let the future and hope of this whole country die? That would be so tragic."

Lark looks to Palla, whose hands are scrambling at the darkness suffocating her, the same way Nightingale had been pulling at her. Her body tenses and releases, over and over.

"There's only two ways she lives," Nightingale says, voice soft. "Either you kill me, or you let me go. Otherwise, I hold this magic as long as I can. You know how long that is. How much longer do you think she can hold her breath? A minute?"

"Couldn't I just knock you out?" Wren asks. "You can't hold the magic then."

"If you're *truly* confident you could do it fast enough," Nightingale sing-songs. "I'm audaciously resilient, I'll warn you."

Lark splutters. "I can't just let you *go*—"

"Well, then you'll have to kill me."

There is a muffled, urgent noise from Palla and it is impossible to tell if she is agreeing or past being able to hear them.

Nightingale smirks. "Except you won't, will you? Hence, the counter offer. I'll even sweeten it for you. Let me go, and she lives. *And* I'll tell you the super secret, incredibly obvious thing you've missed these last two days. It's so obvious, it's hilarious! You just couldn't see it, you funny thing."

Palla's face is changing colour and she is no longer conscious.

"Fine," Lark says, heart pounding while their mind screams with bewilderment, demanding to know what Nightingale is talking about. "Let her go. Then tell me. *Then* Wren will let go of you."

"Promise? Both of you?" Nightingale turns her head to bat her eyelashes at Wren.

Wren meets Lark's eyes, hesitates a moment, and nods. "I promise," she says, and Lark echoes it.

Nightingale smiles and the magic falls away from Palla. The darkness melts into the earth and the smallest of gasps leaves Palla. She does not stir.

Lark dashes to her side, feeling for a pulse. Being a follower of War it is likely Palla has seen many battles, and perhaps even fallen in them and been brought back. If so, resurrection after the first always has a chance of failure. And Palla is too important.

Nightingale coughs impatiently and Lark ignores her. They focus on channelling healing magic into Palla's body, especially trying to get her blood flow back to her brain.

Once convinced that Palla is back on the right track, Lark returns. Their body is shaking with anticipation, protesting the delay in gratification all the way. They fall to their knees again in front of her.

"Alright, what is it?" Lark asks, urgent and fevered, their sense evaporating in the face of Nightingale's taunt. "What did I miss? What is so obvious?"

Nightingale leans in closer and smiles, dazzling and beautiful and the picture of everything wrong in the world. "Oh, Lark. I had help."

Lark blinks.

"You never considered that, did you? That I might be important to anyone but you, because what we have is oh so special." Nightingale sighs. "But, a woman has to live for herself, you know? And these people who helped me escape... oh the plans they have. It's a feat I simply have to see. And they need my expertise."

"*What* expertise?"

"Anything. Everything," Nightingale says with a grin. "I can get it all."

"Fine, fine, who are they, then? Who helped you?" Lark asks.

"Uh uh... let me go, first. You both promised."

Lark and Wren hesitate again. But they did promise, and with another nod from Lark, Wren lets go of Nightingale. Lark stands and pulls Wren to their side immediately.

Nightingale chuckles, stretching her limbs and massaging her purpling neck.

"Thank you," she says, "Well. I suppose I'll be seeing you around."

Lark opens their mouth to argue. They want to tell her that she is wrong, that she cannot just assume that they will follow her, that it is different now because they *see* her and see that she may not be able to come back —

But there is no argument to be made. They cannot let her roam free, especially not now she is part of some strange alliance. Not when this could have all gone differently if Lark had had more conviction.

Have conviction now, a part of them says, but it sounds too much like Palla. *Take her down, here and now. Save countless lives.*

But they cannot kill Nightingale. Not now, not yet. Possibly not ever. And they promised.

"The names, Nightingale," Lark says instead. "Who helped you?"

Nightingale stares, and then laughs as she begins to walk backwards. "Why would I tell you? You not knowing is the best part."

"Nightingale—"

"I told you enough, and I *didn't* promise. You have to watch me, darling, I'm tricky like that." Still walking, she blows them a kiss. "Come try and catch me, yeah? Should be fun. Maybe you'll even solve it, clever thing like you."

Lark rushes forward but it is too late. The portal is made and in a flash, she is a dot on the horizon. In another, out of sight completely.

Chapter 14

DEFEAT TASTES LIKE OLD coffee grounds and sour milk. Betrayal is more like wine turned to vinegar — by what one can only hope is an unfortunate accident but may be sabotage. Between the two, Lark is feeling a strong urge to vomit.

A groan from near Lark brings them back to the immediate and essential. Palla.

They dash back to her side as she stirs. "Are you alright?"

"What happened?" she asks, voice gruff. Her body thrashes and her eyes snap open. "That bitch. Where is she?"

"She's gone. I'm sorry, she was holding you hostage, and everyone keeps saying how important you are, so I couldn't just let you die. I had to let her go."

Palla leaps to her feet. For the first time in months, Lark feels genuine fear for their physical wellbeing — something they are usually too busy to consider. Palla is thunderous. Her aura is filled with so much crimson that it drowns out all other colour, washing her in monochrome as she takes one step forward, and then another.

The arch of the city gate is a large, glorious brick structure. The bricks are a gorgeous pale stone of remarkable integrity and make. Lark admires this workmanship as several ridges of their spine meet it in an unexpected union of Palla's design.

"You let her *go*?!" Palla roars. Her hand is scrunched in their shirt collar where she has them with their feet two inches off the ground. "You had *one job!* I really thought—"

"Ser Palla," Wren says, voice low and quiet but with that unique Wren weight that causes Palla to glance in her direction. "You would have died if we hadn't. We had to make a choice."

"You could have *killed her*!" Palla shouts. "She *said it* and I bet you never even thought of that, did you? Killing her would have cut off the magic and saved me. You have a sword, *you* have magic, you could have killed her in an *instant*! For such a supposed genius you are a useless moron!"

Lark can only stare. There is no excuse that exists that will satisfy her. There is no excuse that exists that will satisfy *them*.

"Ser Palla!" a new voice shouts.

The three of them turn and see Deputy Andrian striding towards them. On his heels are a contingent of city guards and Cillian the admin, who is already surveying the situation with sharp eyes and scribbling furiously.

"Ser Palla," Andrian says, eyeing their current arrangement with a raised eyebrow and nothing more, "report?"

"Your precious Seeker just let her get away," Palla seethes, "that is the report."

"That's *all*? Dear me. Secret sympathy, do you think? Or whimsy?" Cillian asks lightly, quill poised. "Or, *Ser*, is your report, perhaps, incomplete?"

Palla's face gives the impression she would like to render his face incomplete. "They claim it was to save my life. When, obviously, there was a simple way to achieve both but they have no nerve."

"Killing her, you mean?" Andrian asks. No colour swirls around him at all. His face and tone give even less away.

"Obviously."

"I see." Andrian coughs. "I'm sure you can put them down now, Palla."

Palla's grip loosens after a lengthy, petty moment of defiance. Lark reunites with the ground. Before they know it they are next to Wren again, like gravity shifting on instinct.

"This is a very poor show, Lark," Andrian says simply. "How many people will she kill now?"

"I know. But... Palla."

"Yes. Palla." Andrian swallows. "Thank you for ensuring at least she is safe."

Palla fumes. "That is hardly—"

"Hardly what, Palla?" Andrian asks. "Important? In our current times it is essential. Without you the whole *country* may be lost. Lark does not even know the nature of the project and yet they trusted enough in our words to make a call to avoid the worst."

"Tell that to the families of the people she murders now."

"If it means less of them are decimated by dragons in the future, I shall tell them anything necessary."

Lark swallows hard. "I am... truly sorry." They hold the unfathomable gaze of their old classmate and friend. "You really thought I could do this and I've failed far more spectacularly than I ever thought possible." They glance at Cillian, who is still writing furiously. "But trust me when I say that I see now that she may be unreachable. That she needs to be stopped, no matter what."

Andrian sighs. Exhaustion is etched into every line of his face and angle of his body. "I really do hope that is true. I think, however, that what I believed to be a strength is clearly a weakness. Your knowledge of Nightingale may be valuable but hers of you is too much of a detriment. You are not the one to take her down."

Lark stares at Andrian in horror. "She'll kill anyone else who tries."

"She'll try. This war has brought out a number of incredibly skilled mercenaries. With a high enough bounty, I'm sure someone more impartial and just as powerful can manage to eliminate her or bring her in. I think that will be best for everyone."

"Andrian—" Lark licks their lips, twisting their hands in front of them. "I can't just sit by while she's out there."

"I am aware. And as a Seeker, you are free to go where you please and investigate what you like — don't give me that look, Palla, let me finish — and I understand your priorities. However, if you interfere with anyone else's attempt to apprehend her, know you will face significant legal discipline that may not be limited to revocation of your title and Wayfinder."

The silence that follows is heavier than the clouds gathering over the city. The lack of sunlight feels like the last straw, as if it is no longer a rough day but the start of something else altogether.

"I understand," Lark says in the end. "Thank you, Andrian."

"Don't make me regret it."

Lark does not have an answer; they cannot bring themself to promise when the trust they wish they had in themself is just not quite there. They just nod.

"Get in my way again, and I'll crush you," Palla tells Lark, under her breath. "The Bishops won't touch me. These deaths are on you now, and I won't forget."

"You have a good afternoon as well," Lark replies, with a pleasant smile, because everyone else is watching.

Palla snorts and storms off down the street.

"So I'm drafting an emergency bounty, then, Deputy?" Cillian asks. His cheerful manner is grating, insensitive, and Lark has no energy or inclination to do anything but wince at it.

"Time for us to go," Wren says to Andrian and Cillian. "Resupplying for our travels, and all."

"Thank you for your assistance, Wren," Andrian says with a polite smile. "Your presence has been a blessing. Safe travels. Do look after the Seeker for me."

"Of course."

"How are you going to find her, if she got away with that magical blocking thing?" Cillian asks.

Wren bites her lip and glances at Lark. "The Wayfinder is pretty powerful, it should still be able to find her, right? If it can get us close, we'll keep searching the old fashioned way. She's not exactly quiet. Lark? Will the Wayfinder work, if she has the ring?"

Lark blinks. "Oh, uh, I don't know. I am really, truly hoping so. We'll have to try."

Wren's hand slips into Lark's and pulls them into a walk. "Let's go."

Lark is wordless and reeling as they depart from the city gate and make their way back in. Wren passes various stalls and orders fruit and vegetables and dried meat, and finds the closest well to refill their water skins.

"Wren."

Wren is halfway through putting away her change from buying a small wrapper of chocolate, still chuckling from the joke the vendor had made about attracting bees to her flower crown. She looks up, eyes shining, and she is so beautiful that it drives the dagger in Lark's chest several inches deeper. The shame stings.

"Yes?" she asks.

"Wren, you don't have to do this."

"Do what?"

"Follow me into this madness. You didn't sign up for this. You signed up for adventure and exciting new things and helping people."

Wren gives them a funny look. "And helping you catch a murderer *wouldn't* be helping people?"

"Well, no, of course it would but she's so dangerous—"

"So are elementals, and dragons, and creatures infected with rogue magic. That hasn't stopped us before."

Lark is almost beside themself. "We *avoid* dragons, Wren!"

"And I will avoid being murdered." When Lark tries to open their mouth to protest, Wren plants her hand on their shoulder. "Lark. I am not abandoning you. The hold she has over you is terrifying. And unfair. I'm not going to leave you on your own to face it. I'm your friend. And, I have something that I'm really hoping will help us somehow."

Lark stares at her. "What do you mean?"

Wren reaches into her bag and pulls out a handful of crumpled pages of paper. "I managed to tear off some pages from her notebook while I had a hold of her. She's not very strong — only needed one good arm. I can't make sense of the way she writes, but maybe you can?"

The pages indeed hold the shorthand bespoke to Nightingale, the one she had developed when the documentation affliction had begun. Lark had been able to read it at the time, but although familiar still, it is not as easily understood now.

"Perhaps with time," Lark says, glancing up, "it seems to have advanced since I last deciphered it."

"But then we'll have something. Maybe even a clue about who helped her."

Lark is overcome with a maelstrom of emotions so powerful that all they can do is seize Wren in a crushing hug. Wren laughs a moment but quietens after that. She holds them, strong and solid and dependable in measures constantly exceeding expectations.

When they finally break apart, Lark can barely speak but knows their next words are essential.

"You may be the most wonderful person I have ever met."

Wren's cheeks flush. "Um. If you say so?"

"I do. I do. Alright then, time to give chase! We can decipher the pages when we have a spare moment."

They walk until they are out of the city gate, the same one Nightingale left through. Lark pulls the Wayfinder from their bag. The gold circle is heavy enough to demand the strength of both hands. The design is intricate, small sections and switches to be flicked in just the right way to reveal the circumference of engraved runes.

Lark takes a deep breath and traces their fingers around the edges. Step one: focus on the target. Nightingale.

Nightingale, all hair and eyes and secrets and lies. Red. Purple. White. Red. The pain of betrayal and the impossibility of the longing and magnetism. The mind so brilliant, yet so selfish.

Their lips utter the prayer to the Scholar, sealing it with their bespoke verbal key.

"Bring me to that which I seek, or something thereupon."

The magic flares. In their mind's eye the world sprawls before them in a flash of shapes and colour and landscape seen from what could only be a god's eye view. It is less than a moment but glorious. Lark holds their focus tight, keeping it on Nightingale as much as possible. Nightingale, who is now running free, who somehow had *help* —

The world shifts and they are elsewhere.

THE END

Acknowledgments

The first people I want to thank are the ones that encouraged me when I came up with the idea for this series, at least half as a joke because of how absurd and ambitious it was. You know who you are, and thank you for assuring me that "if anyone could pull that off, you could" and encouraging my nonsense.

Lou, Livvy and Beane... y'all are the real ones. Twelve years and counting and we have come so far. I don't know what I would do without you. I could write paragraphs that wouldn't do our friendship justice. Meeting you through our Doctor Who fanfic remains one of the most formative events in my life and I would never trade it for anything.

Ty. My partner, my co-creator, my worldbuilding master, my logic filter who reigns me in when I go too wild... none of this would have been possible without your support or the incredible world you made and let me play in. You make me so fucking happy. I can't wait to show everyone all the other stories we have come up with. Our romances are gonna have people losing their minds.

Sio! The golden retriever to my beagle, it is a delight being silly and dramatic with you and being each other's cheerleaders now and forever.

Kyara and Kai, thanks for always being wonderful. I can't wait to read your books one day!

A huge thanks to my beta readers: Zo, Edith, Rhiannon, Jay, Senka, Harper, Kate, Jen. Your feedback went such a long way to fixing some really crucial details in this story, and polishing many others. Additional thanks to my earliest ARC readers: Ceilidh, Lynea, Nic, Bryanna, Salem. This book is better for your insights. Ceilidh, you especially I want to thank for your boundless and vocal enthusiasm for this series from the moment you started reading it — I needed it desperately at the time, and you gave given me the belief in myself to make sure I finish the race to my first ever publication. Rhiannon, you saved the font size of the paperback with going the extra mile to help me out at a crucial moment. I am SO grateful for your extra support.

To Quinn: thank you for being my editor, and my website designer, and my rock and guide in the self-publishing process. Your helpfulness and practicality have saved me more stress and time than I could begin to measure. Your friendship means a hell of a lot to me.

To the Congregation: you guys (gender neutral) are some of the most wonderful, bonkers, chaotic horny people I have ever had the pleasure to know. Being a part of our Discord has been an incredible experience and I am grateful for you always. Cat,

Harper and Camille, you are closer to the release of the evil goose every day, and I hope that brings you joy.

To Jacqui: thank you for keeping me sane at work, and helping me in countless ways forty hours a week and then some. None of this would have been possible without that!

Additional thanks to anyone who found their way here from my fanfic days, to anyone through my life who supported me and my dream enough to be trusted with this book and my pen name, and to anyone who simply read this book through to the end. I hope you had as much fun as I did, and that you'll want to stick around for the rest of the ride. The chaos is just beginning, I assure you.

For news on upcoming books and exclusive bonus and preview content, sign up to Aimee Donnellan's newsletter!
aimeedonnellan.com/newsletter

For excitable ramblings and musings on the daily, follow Aimee Donnellan on Twitter!
@bardqueenaimee

Any other social media forms are under @aimeedonnellanwrites

The adventure continues in
VOLUME II: THE COLLECTION AWAKENS

Turn the page for a special preview!

Reverie's morning begins with an argument with a goose. Breakfast entertainment — or rather, annoyance — is not something she had ever thought to need, and now that she's had it for six months, she would happily return it.

Unfortunately, fate has other ideas. She and the goose are stuck with each other.

All I'm saying is, once you kill someone the first time, it gets easier, the goose is saying now as she packs the saddlebags and prepares for the day's ride. *So you might as well get it over with.*

Their telepathic link has its uses. But mostly it simply means he can spew bile for her mind only until she commands him to shut up.

"Is this from personal experience?" Reverie asks, out loud so as to not let Melora, her mare, feel left out. "I doubt you ever found it difficult to begin with."

Ferdinand did not begin his lengthy existence as a goose. His previous form had been capable of much greater violence, she has been assured.

Of course I never did, Ferdinand says indignantly. *This is all of your ancestor's nonsense. But if you don't want their advice, then sure.*

"Oh, well if my great-great-great-uncle Stefaric thinks so, then that changes everything! Why didn't you say so?" Reverie exclaims, as if it's a revelation.

Ferdinand lands on the saddlebag while Reverie mounts. Smugness radiates from him as he settles himself as if atop the finest cushion.

A moment later: an almighty, indignant honk.

You're making fun of me! He screeches in her head. *Bitch!*

Reverie pushes him off the horse and relishes the sound of his squawk as he hurtles to the ground and barely catches himself in time. The mare, Melora, snickers. Reverie is not the only one already tired of this company they did not ask for.

The glorious victory is brief. As Reverie turns her eyes ahead, she swallows at the sight of the mountain range that looms before them. Leaving home had been the dream, for several years, and now that it has become reality... she feels so small. So insignificant.

It wasn't supposed to happen this way, she thinks, wistfully.

The mountains cover this part of the border between her home country of Qelandia and Izirm, the Theocracy to the east. Going to the Theocracy had once been an exciting prospect, a country governed by the worshippers of the Higher Pantheon, so familiar yet different to her own Republic and its ruling council.

But then the dragons had attacked. Fear and flame in the air, blood and ash on the ground.

Things can change in a moment. The immovable force of change laughs at the idea of destiny. What a joke.

Reverie glances at the goose, who has resettled himself with a ruffle of feathers and a glare. She squares her jaw and takes a deep breath to calm the seething and poisonous resentment in her chest.

Onward.

Grena's Collection has long lived in her grandmother's stories as a wondrous, peculiar place to visit. *An essential stop for any Rosetia*, she had said. It had always been an eventual, possible destination in the back of her mind. Even nearly a decade on from the last story, every crucial detail remains.

Which is fortunate, given that now, it is the only thing between her and weeks of travel and danger scouring battlegrounds for the family greatsword. No one knows which skirmish took her brother — reliable communication across distance is so difficult without magic, and no one close to her family possesses such an ability.

But all weapons in the Rosetia armoury possess basic enchantments for durability and effectiveness. And anything magical and intriguing may find its way to the Collection.

If she's lucky —

Reverie snorts before finishing the thought. Luck has never been kind to her, but it would be idiotic not to stop by. The Collection is on the way.

The path up the mountain has the audacity to be treacherous and tedious simultaneously. To preserve her sanity and focus, Reverie composes a song about the stormy sky, about lovers meeting under it, braving the wind and rain for each other. By the time it has cohesive lyrics and a halfway decent tune, Reverie is grinning to herself even as her hair is plastered to her head and horns and neck.

Still, poor Melora is drenched. It is a relief to see something ahead that rings a bell in her memory.

"Follow the path up until you find a rock face that looks like a pair of tits," Reverie recites, in Ama's words exactly. Staring at the pair of round rocks with central indents, she has to laugh. "You bitch, it couldn't be a lie, could it? It had to be true. Of course it's true."

Shaking her head with exasperation so powerful it may have turned to bitterness if the whole thing had not been about boob rocks, Reverie presses on. The next part of Ama's directions say to take the sharp left path at this point.

"You're doing so good," Reverie tells Melora, stroking her neck. "I think we're almost there."

Ten minutes on the new path and there is a door pressed into a rockface with the words "Grena's Collection" carved into the rock above it. A manmade alcove is nearby, where two horses are already tied up and grazing on a trough of food. There is room for Melora, so Reverie gets her settled and patted down dry. Three kisses for Melora's nose and a promise to give her some peace from Ferdinand for at least a short while, and Reverie heads inside with the goose on her heels.

A twinkling sound echoes through the room as she steps inside and hangs her soaked green travelling cloak on the rack alongside another. There is no bell above the door. The Collection is windowless and lit only by lamps scattered through the space that is large but somehow still feels cramped.

The items fight for elbow room on every shelf and the aisles are narrow. Directly opposite the door, three signs stand large and important.

Put back everything EXACTLY as you found it, even if purchasing (Grena will sort).

Strictly no violence — noncompliance results in a lifetime ban.

Deposit all magic items in personal storage on the wall (behind you, on the right). No one will be able to open but you. No exceptions, be forthright, Grena will know.

"Control freak?" Reverie asks Ferdinand, quietly. He shrugs with his wings.

"Hey there, traveller!" comes a shout from the back. "Be with you in a hot minute!"

"Awesome, thanks!" Reverie calls back.

There is a magical dagger strapped to one of her thighs, and her mother's non-magical one on the other. Reverie glances at the third sign, locates the personal storage mentioned, and deposits the enchanted one inside.

"Pity I can't fit you in there," she says to Ferdinand.

He cackles. *I bet they're bigger than they look. But you know I won't go quietly.*

It is easy to get lost in the contents of the shelves. There are crystals, jewellery, weapons, tomes and scrolls, and even random household items. None of it seems to be organised by function or appearance, but then, the magical function of objects is not always immediately clear.

Reverie's eyes are caught by a teapot with green vines painted all across the fine ceramic. Her fingers trace over the smooth surface as nostalgia bubbles in her chest, sauntering away to afternoon tea on the lawn with her mother. *She'd love this*, Reverie thinks. But she has no budget for any frivolous gifts. Magic is expensive and she is here for one thing only.

With a sigh, she releases the teapot and stands still long enough to realise she is dripping onto the carpet.

"Shit," she mutters, and steps outside again for a moment to squeeze out both of her braids in an attempt to wring some water out.

The sun is setting and thunder is beginning to crackle outside. Reverie is glad to duck back into the Collection for now.

Upon returning, she spots Ferdinand perched on top of a tall shelf. A dusty suit of armour stands proudly in front of it — but not for long. Ferdinand glances back at her and gives his equivalent of a smirk.

Before Reverie can shout any command that will magically stop him in his conniving tracks, the goose has launched himself at the shoulders and helmet of the armour. It crashes to the floor with a sound so awful that a nearby woman bursts into tears.

Reverie runs around the shelves to reach her. "Shit. I'm so sorry, he's such an asshole. Are you okay?"

The woman is shaking from head to toe and runs her hands over her long brown hair, tucking it behind her partially pointed ears.

"I — yeah. Yeah, I'm okay. I just wasn't expecting... is that a goose?"

Ferdinand is honk-cackling with delight. *Damn, she's crying? This is the best day ever.*

"Is he... laughing at me?" the woman asks, bewildered.

"Shut up and sit still," Reverie commands Ferdinand, and the magic of their bond forces him to sit on top of the armour's back and keep his beak shut.

"What the hell was that? Was that my armour?" the voice from before calls out.

"Uh. Yeah. Sorry!"

"Put it back *exactly* where it was! Now!"

Reverie hurries to do so but cannot stop herself muttering mocking imitations of the words under her breath.

"Wait," the voice says. "Ferdinand! Is that you, you little asshole?"

Heads whip in unison to process the figure who has zoomed into view at the end of the aisle. Her hair is silvery blue and seems to be attempting to announce independence from her head by reaching as far from her scalp as the curls can manage. Her gnomish stature puts her at eye level with Ferdinand as she strides up to him.

"Same audacious size," she says, and her eyes — entirely black, like glassy orbs, potentially a sign of demon blood in her lineage or something similar — flick to Reverie. "And companion to a golden horned traveller with skin *that* shade of pink. Yep. Same goose."

Reverie tilts her head. "Oh! So you... know my grandmother, then?"

"Amalina is a regular customer, every few years or so," the blue haired gnome says with a grin, "I love her. Best stories. What a woman. In small doses."

"Small doses for sure," Reverie says, forcing a smile and trying to scrounge up enough bullshit to form a convincing